THE WOMAN WHO NEVER DID

and a circle of short stories

by

Jenefer Heap

Copyright © Jenefer Heap 2015

The right of Jenefer Heap to be identified as the author of this work has been asserted by her in accordance with the Copyright, Designs and Patents Act 1988.

All rights reserved.
No part of this publication may be reproduced, stored in a retrieval system, distributed, or transmitted in any form or by any means (including photocopying, recording, or other electronic or mechanical methods) without the prior written permission of the copyright holder, except in the case of brief quotations and certain other non-commercial uses permitted by copyright law.

All characters in this book are fictitious and any resemblance to any person, living or dead, is purely co-incidental.

First published in 2015

www.jeneferheap.wordpress.com

ISBN-10: 1517327539
ISBN-13: 978-1517327538

This book is dedicated to my father

Donald Rosser

1932-2015

Contents

The Woman Who Never Did	1
Gloria	11
Felicia's Souk	23
Belvedere Road	39
The Green Tie	57
The Spoiler of the Fun	65
A Game of Pirates	77
Room 516	87
The Man in the Shadows	97
The View from the Penthouse Apartment	109
Gingerbread	121

Incident at the Copper Kettle Tea Rooms	145
The Wish Child	167
Vanessa Chesterton's Wishes	185
The Burning Girl	199
Author's note	
Acknowledgements	

The Woman Who Never Did

Connie gazed out of her bedroom window and wondered how her life might have been if she had become a poet. Would the weary, homeward-bound commuters blaze to life in the fiery sunset, or crumble to ash in the long evening shadows? Would the comfortable, middle-aged couples strolling to dinner pause to reignite their passion in the golden evening glow? Was the Italian restaurant across the square engulfed in an inferno – or was the window simply aflame with reflected light that dazzled Connie, awakening a vaguely remembered pain?

The clock in the square struck seven and she turned her thoughts towards the less unsettling question of what to wear to the book group. The other women were always so perfectly turned out, so precisely themselves. Barbara (retired headmistress) wore crisp sit-up-straight blouses and a no-nonsense single strand of pearls. Marcia (serial internet-dater) dressed less formally 'Ten Years Younger' in boot-cut jeans and long-line leather jacket. Jean (fewer candlelit dinners, but a lot more sex) was up-front in low-necked Lycra. Terri (Business Woman of the Year 1989) power-dressed to perfection with her mobile phone at the ready. If Rosemary (poor Rosemary) felt well enough to attend, she'd wear a designer leisure suit, illness was no excuse to abandon style.

But what about Connie (widow, and full-time mother – retired). She looked at the flowery skirt and trademark turtleneck hanging on the wardrobe door, shades of beige against the mahogany. She'd never been drawn to a big career like Terri's or felt a vocation like Barbara's. Ten years a widow, she had no desire for romance and was pleased to forget about sex altogether. Unlike Rosemary, thank God, she was still in pretty good health – the bottle of pills she kept by the bed for emergencies hadn't been touched for months. Nothing to remark upon, was that what her clothes said about her?

After Graham rescued her from drowning in his typing pool, likening her cropped blonde hair and lovely legs to Doris Day, Connie had settled effortlessly into domesticity. For some years they lived in a spacious family villa in the Oxfordshire countryside, downsizing to a period house in town after Sarah and Becky left home. There had been talk of retirement and a new nomadic life, but everyone knew Graham would have to be carried out of the boardroom feet first and, two weeks before his sixty-fifth birthday, he was. Since then, Connie's daughters (their own lives overflowing with families, careers, and causes) had campaigned to persuade their mother to 'get out more' – belly-dancing perhaps, or a country weekend break with life drawing classes. Connie felt these were strange suggestions from her conventionally minded off-spring (in many ways the girls were so like their father), but they belonged to a generation of women encouraged to believe they could do it all. To them, she thought, I'm just the woman who never did.

How came children to know so much better than their mothers? Connie picked up a framed photograph: two little girls paddling on a Cornish beach. How biddable they had been back then. When did the shift in power begin? When they left home or got their first job? When their own children were born? She considered the younger Connie in the picture: turtleneck and shorts, hair the same practical crop she still wore. Perhaps it was some shift in her: Menopause? Widowhood? Or had it started with marriage? Graham wasn't in the holiday snap. He rarely was; Graham never would trust her with the camera.

THE WOMAN WHO NEVER DID

Connie had to squint at the photograph, the sunset was fading. Where had all that time gone? She changed into her top and skirt, freshened her makeup and fastened the gold watch Graham had bought for her fiftieth. A quick check in the mirror – Connie looked the same, but she felt a little different. Perhaps tonight would be different. She picked up her well-thumbed copy of the book – tonight she had something to say.

The clock was striking eight as Connie slipped across the square and down the mews to Marcia's cottage. She had joined the book group to pacify her daughters, but found she rather enjoyed sitting in cosy surroundings with a glass of wine and carrot stick dips, listening to the other women give their views on the latest from Hilary Mantel or Kazuo Ishiguro. Each member had assumed their natural role within the group, such as literary historian or Devil's advocate; Connie's being that of polite listener.

She rang the doorbell and waited between the potted tulips, listening to the rhythm of the chatter within. Jean opened the door.

'Come on in, sweetheart. We're just about to start. I saved you a place.' She handed over a glass of Chablis and led the way through to the tiny sitting room, where they squeezed next to Marcia on an undersized sofa that was already crowded with scatter cushions in fashionable spring hues. Barbara sat poker straight on a dining chair, while Terri laid claim to the hearth rug, the single easy chair being reserved for poor Rosemary.

Terri pulled the chosen book from her expensively simple tote and Connie felt a crackle of excitement. 'I chose Ron Birch's *The Burning Girl*. Out of print for years. Recently rediscovered by Hollywood. Movie premiers this weekend,' Terri spoke as though addressing a meeting of time-pressed underlings. 'The book documents the social displacement of a free-spirited teenaged girl in 1950s Britain and the catastrophic events this brings about. Birch was on Film Talk last night and I've brought a recording along for us to watch. So what did we think?'

Connie took a breath, but Jean got in first. 'Well, it's a bit dated, but some of the imagery was wonderful. That bit where she's up on the roof while the school burns. They've made it into a fantastic poster for the film.'

'It's an iconic image.' Terri held up the book, displaying the front cover, a startling picture of a young girl, hair on fire, posed like a crucifix on the roof of a burning school. 'The girl herself, Birch doesn't give her a name — heroine or villain?'

Ex-headmistress, Barbara, was adamant. 'Undoubtedly she's the villain. Burning down the school library is quite simply an act of scholastic terrorism.'

Marcia leapt to the girl's defence. 'But surely we must feel sympathy. Her family background. Those dreadful psychiatrists.'

Jean was quick with her indignation. 'Oh, ECT was a common enough treatment for difficult females in those days. Petty crime, civic disobedience, postnatal depression even – zap a few volts through 'em. Quieten the silly women down.'

'Shocking!' Terri commented with a smirk. The other members of the book group all turned to look sternly at her over their spectacles.

Rosemary's tone was friendly but firm, 'It's nothing to laugh about, Terri. I've read about ECT and there are some very distressing accounts. The treatment's bad enough, but the after effects! Memory loss, confusion. Some people even said that afterwards a part of their personality was gone forever. It may have quietened the silly women down, as Jean so succinctly puts it, but at a terrible cost.'

'And hasn't it been linked to suicide?' Marcia added, 'Like *The Burning Girl* herself?'

Jean snorted, 'Well I say she's a heroine.'

And so the conversation went on. Connie listened and wondered when she should join in. The other women covered the whole of Ron Birch's book in detail. They found plenty to discuss from the limited opportunities for women of the period (Terri) to the changes in the British education system since the 1950s (Barbara). They watched the Film Talk interview. Birch was looking good for a man in his late sixties and that started them on another thread. Still Connie said nothing.

After Barbara had given her verdict on the symbolism and language of *The Burning Girl* and Connie had still not spoken, the conversation began to diverge. Jean and Rosemary talked about the new superstore. Terri checked her mobile phone. Marcia disappeared into the kitchen for more wine.

Barbara leaned across to Connie. 'You've been very quiet this evening. What did you think?'

'I was at school with Ron Birch.' Connie spoke so softly she thought they might not hear.

But she had everyone's attention at last. Marcia reappeared, without the bottle, and perched on the arm of the sofa. 'Was he handsome?'

'Very handsome, but ...'

Barbara was next. 'Was his literary talent recognised at school? I'm sure I read something about a poetry prize...' She picked up a copy of *The Burning Girl* and turned to the author's biography.

'There was a poetry prize, but someone else won that. I ...'

'Oh, come on, Connie.' Terri interrupted, 'Tell us about the girl. Birch said she was based on someone at school. Did you know her?'

Connie spoke slowly, 'I knew her. Ron spent a lot of time with her that summer. I suppose they were in love.'

'What was she like?' Rosemary asked gently. 'Were you friends?'

'She was full of life and very bright. Everyone said she was wild, but I don't think they knew her well.'

Barbara wanted to know 'Did she really set fire to the school library?'

'Not the library. It was the headmaster's study. And he wasn't a very nice man.' A light flickered in Connie's eyes then quietened down again.

Jean leaned forward into the thick of the conversation. 'Was the rest true – did she stand on the school roof with her hair on fire? Did they give her ECT?'

Connie's fingers found her own cropped hair then lingered at the throat of her turtleneck. 'We all had long hair in those days. Afterwards, they took her away somewhere. I don't really remember. It was such a long time ago.'

'And in the end?'

'Did she commit suicide?'

'What happened to her? Do you know?'

Their questions rubbed like dry sticks in Connie's brain but no spark came, only a dull, vaguely remembered pain. She took a breath. 'I expect she settled down and got married. Like we all did.'

Connie said little more and the conversation fizzled out. Barbara rounded off the discussion by thanking Terri for her stimulating choice of book and Marcia for providing the delicious wine and nibbles. Jean suggested that, for their next read, the group revisit *Fear of Flying* to make a comparison with *Fifty Shades of Grey*.

Then the ladies talked of other things.

The clock in the square struck eleven as the members of the book group said goodnight. The last of the candles flickered in the window of the Italian restaurant. Connie watched Jean's pink stilettos tottering off up the road, then stood a while in the square gazing up at her bedroom window as she thought about the things she hadn't done, and wondered how her life might be, if she became a poet.

Gloria

I had a bit of a chuckle on the way home from the book group. Barbara's face when I suggested *Fear of Flying* and *Fifty Shades of Grey*! What an old biddy – and she's only a couple of years older than I am. Well, Barbara mightn't approve, but I fully intend to hang onto my libido to the bitter end.

    I thought about popping in the Red Lion, but it was nearly closing time, plus I'd had a glass too much book group plonk and my gorgeous new shoes were killing me. So I headed straight for home. I let myself in the front door, squeezed past the double buggy in the hall (it's always in the way, but young Saffron on the ground floor has her hands full with the twins and they're such nice little kiddies) and hauled myself up the two flights to my flat. Our purpose-built block looks as out of place in the old town as a nose-ring on a nun, but I'm not the cottagey sort. No bric-a-brac and silver framed family snaps for me. I'm more your black and white photo art and glass-topped table type. Minimalist, except for the wall to wall books. Still, the flat can feel a bit empty after dark and it seemed terribly quiet when I got in. So I poured myself a nice little bedtime brandy and I was just getting into my nightie when I noticed the light flashing on the answer machine.

'You have two new messages. First message: Hello Jean. You coming in the Lion tonight? Moira's staying over at her sister's.'

Half an hour too late, Ted Potts! I'd already taken my makeup off and nobody sees that part of me naked.

'Second message: Jean? It's Gloria. I'm in Southampton till Saturday. I'd love to see you – any chance we can catch up? You can reach me on...'

Well! I poured another, bigger, brandy, sat down and picked up the TV remote. That lispy interviewer was on, full of himself but good for a laugh. Usual chat show fodder: beautiful young actress, comedian making good in US, ex-politician turned porn star – or was it pop star?

I turned the TV off, drained the brandy, and played the message again.

'Jean? It's Gloria. I'm in Southampton till Saturday. I'd love to see you ....'

GLORIA

After ten years, Gloria? And why would I want to see you? I turned off all the lights and went straight to bed.

I tossed and turned for an hour or so then went to look for something to read. Hilary Mantel or a trusty *Black Lace*? I wasn't really in the mood for either. I put the radio on for a bit of company, but at that time of night it's all lonely lost souls. After a while I gave up, got up, opened my wardrobe and started pulling out all my best clothes. But what exactly do you wear for a dinner date with the woman who lured away the love of your life?

It was getting on for twenty years since I last set foot in the Mermaid Hotel. Dan and I used to drink there in the old days. It looked pretty much the same from the outside, but inside it was all cocktail bar and chrome. Mind you, their rooms must have been in a time warp – hotel beige with a bit of brown for contrast. I unpacked my trolley case, fixed myself a G&T from the mini-bar and had a lie down on the bed.

I still hadn't spoken to Gloria, just left her a message to book dinner for Thursday night. I didn't want to think about her, but I couldn't stop myself thinking about Dan. My Danny, six foot of beautiful. These days he'd have been modelling for Ralph Lauren. Back then he was just a salesman – but he looked like a film star. We'd walk into any room and all the heads would turn, and it wasn't me they were

GLORIA

looking at, even though I was quite something in those days – not exactly a beauty, but damn sexy. But Danny, now he was more than sexy. With his pale blue eyes and dusty blonde hair he was in another league. It did your soul good just to look at him. His mum told me once how she used to love pushing him in his pram and watching the smiles light up on people's faces when they saw him. Our babies would have been so bonny, but Dan was in no hurry and I never pushed it. It was enough that my Danny loved me – that made my life beautiful.

Gin does get me a bit weepy sometimes, but I pulled myself together again and had a walk into the town centre for a bit of retail therapy. Thought I might find the perfect killer outfit for dinner, something classy like Gloria might wear. There were a couple of possibles in Debenhams, but, however high the price tag, on me they just looked bargain basement. All the time I was keeping an eye out, wondering if Gloria was shopping too. I sat in the window of Costa with a cappuccino and a bit of shortbread. Got chatting to a young girl with a pushchair and made some funny faces to cheer her kiddie up. Nice girl. Said she bet I was fantastic with my own grandkids.

I went back to the Mermaid to put my feet up for an hour or two, but I couldn't settle there either. So I had a rummage in the mini-bar, opened one of those little bottles of wine, and watched *Countdown*. I started

GLORIA

getting ready too early, tried on everything I'd brought with me over and over until I had to ring down for an iron and start again. The only thing I was sure of was my gorgeous shoes. When you're only five foot two and about to square up to an Amazon you need a serious heel – besides a girl always feels better with a bit of diamante.

Just after seven o'clock I blotted my lipstick, sprayed a mist of something musky, and admired the results in the mirror: fuchsia wrap top – my signature colour with a nice deep V; black pencil skirt – classic, but sexy; shoes – gorgeous, obviously. I had done a cracking job.

To boost my confidence, I had a G&T in the hotel bar and bit of a flirt with an aging yachtsman who was stopping over on his way to Cowes: 'You're looking very lovely, my dear, I hope your gentleman friend appreciates you.'

Then I set off to meet Gloria.

Spinnakers was a new restaurant set in the city walls. In my day it was a spit and sawdust pub. Now it was all understated, overpriced elegance, exclusively designed for people with more money than sense. There was a big twisted glass chandelier and a specky youth sat at a piano playing dumbed-down jazz.

Gloria was waiting at a table for two by the window. She stood up to greet me, azure silk jersey draping elegantly as she held out her arms, film star smile at the ready. I sidestepped the embrace and got

GLORIA

a waft of perfume (subtle and citrusy), and a glimpse of the gold bracelet I bought her all those years ago. We manoeuvred through the cheek kissing with a bit of awkward stooping and stretching.

'This looks classy.' I sniffed, looking around the restaurant. It looked pricey too but even midweek it was full of diners.

'The ship's purser recommended it. The city's changed so much I wouldn't have known where to go.' Gloria said as we sat down. 'It's lucky we booked.'

Lucky? Lucky our chairs were at right angles so I didn't have to look her in the face.

'So, Gloria,' I asked from behind the menu, 'is this your first time back in Southampton?'

'Not the first, but I haven't been ashore much. What shall we have? It's so good to see you, Jean. Shall we have champagne?'

'Aren't you the diva these days! It'd be wasted on me. I'll stick with the house red.'

Gloria flushed and I chalked one up to me, but it didn't feel good. I didn't really know how to feel. I'd been prepared for battle and part of me still wanted to slap her, but another part wanted a cuddle. So I got stuck into the wine instead.

Couldn't tell you what we ate, something fishy. Gloria rattled on about life on the cruise ships. She'd always had a cracking voice for karaoke and there she was living the dream, crooning out torch songs for the rich oldies on the high seas. I guzzled my way

GLORIA

through two bottles as I listened to her gush, all the time waiting for just one mention of Dan.

I've never had a head for red. It makes me blotchy and belligerent. And randy. Of course at the time I think I'm completely irresistible, especially to handsome young waiters who think they might be in with the chance of a good tip. I can't remember all the details, but I do remember explaining in a loud voice to the whole restaurant exactly what I'd like on a plate for pudding and where I'd be squirting the whipped cream. Gloria tried to get me to quieten down a bit, but I told her she was the last person I'd take a lecture from. Then, and sadly I do remember this, as the waiter cleared the plates I gave his bum a playful pinch. And I also remember the pretty young waitress who charged across the restaurant and chucked the dregs of my wine in my face.

'Keep your wrinkly hands to yourself!'

The manager hurried over. 'Ladies, ladies! Linda, what on earth are you doing?'

They all started talking at once. The manager was apologising to me, the waitress was shouting at the manager, the waiter was shouting at the waitress. And everyone else in the restaurant was enjoying the floorshow.

The manager's face was brighter than my wrap top. 'That's enough, Linda – you're fired.'

Gloria held up her hands trying to calm things down. 'Please … It's just a misunderstanding. There's no need to fire anybody.'

GLORIA

Wiping red wine from my cheeks, I slurred my agreement.

'That's very understanding, madam. Linda, apologise to the ladies then go and calm down.'

'Ladies? That sad old bag's the oldest slapper in town!' She spat the words at me, then turned on Gloria.

'And Lofty here looks like a man in drag!'

The waitress was fired, the bill was waived, anything to get us out of there quickly and quietly. Gloria helped me back to the Mermaid – my gorgeous shoes were trying to take me in two different directions at once. She ordered coffee in the chrome cocktail lounge, which was blissfully deserted after the restaurant, and we sat down at a table in the corner.

'Goodness, Jean, this place has changed. Where are the saggy old armchairs? Do you remember the time –'

'Oh shut it, Gloria. I'm not in the mood for small talk.'

She shut it. The barman brought our coffees over. When I looked up Gloria was dabbing her eyes with a hanky.

'I'm sorry,' I said. 'Some things never change. I'm still scrapping like an alley cat and you're the pedigree Persian.' I looked her fully in the face for the first time and Danny's beautiful blue eyes looked back at me.

GLORIA

'It's just that I miss you ... I miss him so much.' I looked away, Gloria took hold of my hand and I started crying too. 'Don't you miss him?'

'Sometimes. But Danny was never real, Jean. He was like a mask I had to wear. It was such a relief to take it off.'

I nearly did slap her then. 'A mask? I was happily married to that mask for fifteen years. Fifteen years and then your mum dies and suddenly everything we've got is a lie?'

With a giddying rush my head filled with memories. The day Dan revealed his big secret, the hidden tragedy of his life. All the psychology and the science I read up on till I knew even more about gender dysphoria than he did. The times I reminded myself it was all to do with hormones. Decided in the womb. Nobody's fault, no reflection on me – on either of us. I tried to put myself in his place, helped him, supported him, listened to him. Because I believed any scrap of Danny I could keep hold of would be worth it. I held his hand through the counselling, the hormone treatments, the beauty treatments, the whole bloody lot. I even helped create Gloria – clamped my knees tight shut on my own needs and made myself into her best friend. Then after all that, after all the hopes and plans I'd turned my back on, Gloria waved goodbye and set off to pursue her dream. And my Danny was gone forever.

GLORIA

When they left, something bloated and boiling burst inside me and I ran from the whispers and the nudges and those pitying looks I'd put up with for so long. I ran away from the city where everyone knew me and Dan and Gloria. I found my own fresh start and I unclamped my knees for anyone I wanted. For any man who wanted me. Not as a friend or a counsellor – as a woman. And I found a life again. A life with a bit of happiness in it for me.

'Oh, Gloria, why did you call? Why after ten years did you call me now?' Tears were running down my face, but I needed to know.

Tears were running down Gloria's as she answered me. 'I missed you, Jean. I miss my best friend. I could never have done it without you. You were amazing.'

'Oh yeah. The archetypal tart with a heart.'

'And a brain. A good one when you chose to use it.'

'I've always thought there's more fun to be had without thinking.'

Gloria gave a little smile. 'Like tonight?'

'I was bang on form, wasn't I?' I caught my ravaged reflection in the chrome fittings. 'When did I get so old and ugly?'

'We're all getting older. But you'll never be ugly.'

I took a deep breath, 'Do you ever regret it? All the treatment, all the trauma. Do you ever regret it, Danny?'

GLORIA

'Gloria.' She said it gently but firmly. 'No, darling. Je ne regrette rien.'

'But after ten years you still miss me.' My fingers brushed against her bracelet and I tangled them in its golden links. 'Come up to bed with me now. We don't have to do anything. We could just hold each other and go to sleep.' I held my breath.

'I can't, Jean. I can't give you what you want. I'm sorry.'

'Danny was the love of my life.'

'I know,' she said softly. 'And I'll always love you, Jean.'

With trembling fingers I untwined the bracelet, but kept hold of Gloria's hand. Then, at last, I let go.

We didn't drag it out. I walked back outside with Gloria and watched her glide away down the street with more poise than I've managed in my entire life. Then I teetered back into The Mermaid, cold, wrung out and needing a pee. I sat in a cubicle in the Ladies' feeling like a ninety-year-old granny – but that was something I never would be.

All the same, I couldn't sit sobbing on the loo all night. So I got out my compact and fought that sad old bag into submission with a bit of lippy and mascara. Then, as I was collecting my key from reception, the ancient mariner wandered past.

'Back so soon, dear lady? The evening is still young. Won't you join me for a drink in the bar?'

GLORIA

Well why the hell not? I said to myself. And I put on my brightest smile.

'Don't mind if I do. But there's not much atmosphere in there, sweetie. Let's have a nightcap in my room instead.'

Felicia's Souk

In the middle of the night, in the middle of the city, in the middle of a park, on a weathered wooden bench, a pretty girl was crying. She was all alone, deep, deep in the foresty dark, far from the streetlamp-lit grey roads that framed the fairytale landscape of grass and trees.

The girl was mostly dressed in black, which helped her to hide in the dark. Her shoes, her stockings, her dress were all black, and a soft black scarf was pulled up around her head. Her mood was black too and she muttered an incantation as she rocked to and fro.

'Stupid stupid stupid stupid stupid...'

FELICIA'S SOUK

Weary of rocking and crying, the girl in black tugged at her white apron to wipe her tears. As she did so, the scarf around her head fell away, and her long golden plait gleamed in the sudden moonlight. The girl was more than pretty. And, despite her chant, she was far from stupid.

At the far end of the park a woman screamed. 'My bag! My bag!'

The girl jumped up from the bench and picked up a stout stick. A hooded figure hurtled along the path towards her and she gave a furious roar, swung the stick and hit at its belly. The hooded figure stumbled and the girl snatched back the stolen bag as a flash of purple light knocked her off her feet and she watched, dazed, as the thief fled through the trees.

Old lady hands gently took hold of the capacious silver bag and helped the girl stand up. 'Are you hurt, my dear?'

'I don't think so.' She brushed herself down. 'That flash? Did you see it?'

'I saw that you are a very brave and resourceful girl. Thank you, my dear, for rescuing my bag. It's a faithful old companion. I should hate to lose it.'

The girl looked down at the old lady with the silvery hair and twinkling violet eyes.

'Are you alright?' she asked softly. 'The park really isn't safe at night. We should probably call the police. I didn't see his face, but I think I'd recognise that purple hoodie.'

'I'd rather get home, I feel a little shaken. Perhaps you would walk with me?' The old lady took hold of the girl's arm. 'We can talk on the way. You can tell me why you were crying all alone in the dark. And why there is no handsome prince here to protect you.'

The girl laughed. 'If only I could meet a handsome prince! All the guys I know are scumbags.' And together they walked out of the shadowy park to the brightly lit streets of the city.

They talked as they walked arm in arm. The old lady's touch was strangely comforting, and the girl found herself telling all her troubles, which had been so distressing, but suddenly seemed unimportant.

'It's funny,' said Linda, for that was the girl's name. 'I thought I was so in love. Now I can't think what I ever saw in him.'

'He does sound a very handsome young man,' the old lady replied. 'But vain and rather shallow. And how unsavoury to flirt with that elderly woman for pecuniary motives.'

'I'm better off without him. I know I shouldn't have chucked wine over a customer, but I just saw red. I don't care about being sacked either. I didn't really like being a waitress.' Linda sighed. 'But I still need to pay the rent.'

'Perhaps I can help you there, my dear.' The old lady's violet eyes glittered a deeper purple.

FELICIA'S SOUK

Felicia's Souk was one of a row of interesting little shops in a side street on the edge of the city centre. From outside it appeared tiny but enticing. Inside it wound forever deeper, up and down little flights of stairs, each corner packed with nearly-new delights. Linda was fascinated by the alluring displays of expensive clothes, designer accessories, and classy knick-knacks.

The old lady explained the ethos of her shop as she gave her new assistant a tour. 'The rich donate their unwanted belongings. We sell them and keep half to cover the running costs. The rest of the money is donated to their chosen charity.'

'That sounds like an awful lot of admin,' Linda observed.

'Oh, it's not too difficult, my dear. I have my own system. Not on a computer — goodness no! I wouldn't give those dreadful things the time of day. I have a more ... old-fashioned way of doing things.'

'Felicia's Souk is a very pretty name — are you Felicia?'

'Felicia Gildenfleur. But it's such a mouthful. Call me FG, everyone does.'

'My name's a bit of a mouthful too. Linda Popetanovski. No one can say it let alone spell it!'

'Ah, but it is a very old and distinguished name. The Kokovanian royal family were Popetanovskis. A great and noble line. Why, in the old days...' The old woman's face was fleetingly sad. 'But of course you've never heard of Kokovania. Ah well, few have these days.'

'It sounds like a French chicken dish.' Linda laughed, adding wistfully, 'I don't have any family, let alone a royal one. I never knew my parents.'

FG smiled sympathetically. 'Then, my dear, since you may well be descended from royalty, we must find you a prince.'

Linda loved working for the old lady with the twinkling violet eyes and mysterious smile. Each day at Felicia's Souk was full of exciting discoveries. FG bustled to and fro working her magic, searching out the perfect dress for a Goth's graduation ball, or an antique puzzle box to hold a diamond eternity ring. The more desperate the search, the more thrillingly perfect the find.

Then, towards the end of Linda's first week, an amazing thing happened. She rushed into the office, a little room at the back of the shop that should have been stuffy and damp, but always smelt of freesias and fresh air. FG looked up from a large ledger bound in purple leather and let her half-moon glasses dangle from their silver chain.

'My dear, you look all of a fluster. Sit down and catch your breath.'

Linda perched on the edge of a chair. 'Oh, FG, I've got a date! He came in to drop off a couple of bags of clothes for his mum and we got chatting. He's asked me to a ball on Saturday! He's ever so nice. And ever so posh.' Her smile vanished. 'But the ball's tomorrow and I haven't got anything to wear!'

'Perhaps I can help you there, my dear.' FG tucked her glasses away in her silver handbag. 'It sounds very exciting. What is the young man's name?'

'Hugo Something-or-Other. It's as unpronounceable as mine.'

'Hugo Romoli-Boronowskov? I know his mother. Delightful young man, quite good looking. Well, he certainly is posh, and wealthy too. The Romoli-Boronowskovs are old-world aristocracy. I believe his father was the son of a prince. You will need something extra special.'

It was a quiet afternoon in Felicia's Souk, so Linda and FG were able to devote themselves to finding the perfect dress. There were dozens to choose from, but none was quite right. Many were simply too big, or wrongly proportioned for Linda's petite frame. The few that were a good fit were too sombre or too garish. Linda began to panic, and even FG looked perplexed.

'Put the kettle on, my dear. I'll have one last look in the stockroom. Perhaps we missed something.'

Linda knew they'd searched every rail, shelf and box in the shop and her heart was heavy as she arranged bourbons and custard creams on a china plate and waited for the kettle to boil. She noticed a flickering purple light under the stockroom door and made a mental note that the fluorescent tube was faulty. But all thoughts of faulty lights, or even tea and biscuits, were forgotten when FG reappeared in triumph, carrying a beautiful silver and lilac ball gown.

Linda gasped. 'Where did you find it?'

FG steered her towards the changing room. The girl stood mesmerised before the mirror as nimble fingers fastened two dozen dainty silver buttons. The fit was perfect, the cut demure. A dainty filigree choker completed the ensemble.

'Oh, it's wonderful! But how...?'

The old lady loosened the girl's plait and golden hair tumbled over her shoulders. 'You will need shoes. Your feet are so small I think these may fit.' She held out a dainty pair of silver satin bridesmaid shoes decorated with tiny lilac crystals.

Linda slipped on the shoes and turned to the old lady with tears in her eyes. 'Do I scrub up well?'

'You look like a princess, my dear. A true Popetanovski – fit to grace the Grand Ballroom at the Crystal Palace of Kokovania. Wear it on Saturday and bring it back next week. Now, you must take tomorrow off and save your energy for dancing.' She waved away the girl's protests. 'Not another word. Tell me all about it on Monday.'

On Monday morning, over a cup of tea and a jammy dodger, Linda told FG all about the ball.

'It was very grand. Hugo sent a chauffeur to collect me. And he met me at the door with a purple orchid for my dress. Everything was so beautiful, the house, the grounds... There were tables and tables of delicious food, and I drank champagne all evening.'

'Did you dance the night away?'

'I danced a couple of dances with Hugo and then I danced with some other guys. It wasn't really my sort of music.' Linda gave a little shrug. 'To be honest, it was all a bit dull. And so much expensive food and drink! I felt quite uncomfortable about it ... I mean when you see how little some people have ...' She picked up a charity leaflet from FG's desk and considered it thoughtfully before continuing. 'Hugo was ever so nice – but rather stuffy. He called on Sunday morning to ask me out again. But I put him off.'

'Ah well, the Romoli-Boronowskov's always did have weak chins.' FG sighed. 'Charming, but the wrong prince.'

Linda sighed too. 'Fraid so.' Then she giggled. 'Oh, but, FG, something really embarrassing happened when I was getting ready for the ball. Did I tell you my flat's up on the tenth floor so it's not overlooked? Well, I'd just got out of the shower, and I was wandering about in the nude. And then this builder walked past my window!'

'Walked past your window?' FG frowned. 'How could that be?'

'He was on one of those cradle things, hanging from the roof.' Linda giggled again. 'I shouted at him and dived down behind the sofa. But he must have got an eyeful!'

'How embarrassing,' the old lady agreed, absently. 'Tell me, my dear, what exactly is your sort of music?'

Two days later another amazing thing happened. Emerging from her office, FG found Linda deep in conversation with a young man in an immaculately tailored white leather jacket. The man flashed a showbiz smile as he tapped the last few digits of Linda's phone number into his electric-blue iPhone.

'Laters, Linz. I'll send a car.' He picked up a small carrier bag and with a salute to FG he was gone.

'I think I recognise that young man. But it's very hard to tell through those dark glasses,' the old lady remarked with raised eyebrows.

'Oh, FG. That's Dax Lennox. D...D...Dax Lennox was here in the shop! Buying a belt,' Linda stammered breathlessly. 'From me!'

'Dax *Who* was buying a belt?'

'Dax Lennox – The Prince Regent of Pop. You must have heard his latest, *Déjà Days* – it's on the radio all the time. He's playing Wembley tonight! I tried to get tickets but they'd sold out in minutes. Oh, FG, you'll never guess...'

'Then you'd better tell me.'

Linda did a little dance. 'He's invited me to go as his guest!'

'His guest? How wonderful,' FG exclaimed with a smile. 'What will you wear?'

'Tea, how lovely. Thank you my dear.' FG cleared a space on her desk. 'Let's have a ginger nut too. And you can tell me all about the concert.'

Linda sat down. 'The concert was great. Thanks for helping with my outfit – the leather trousers and purple boots were perfect. And that gorgeous silver top – can I put it aside till pay day?'

'Of course. But how was the evening? And how was the dashing Dax Lennox?' FG smiled encouragingly.

'He was a bit boring really.' Linda sighed. 'All he could talk about was music. And I don't know a thing about music – I just like listening to it. Plus under those dark glasses and the beautiful jacket he was a bit weedy, not my type at all. And …' she lowered her voice, 'I think he might have addiction issues, there was all sorts of stuff lying about.' She brightened, 'The concert was amazing though. He brought me out on stage in front of all those people and sang *Déjà Days* just to me!'

FG looked sternly over the top of her glasses. 'Well we certainly can't have you getting involved with drugs. You won't be seeing Dax Lennox again.'

'No. He asked me to go over for the Munich concert next week. But I didn't think it would be fair to accept. He's not really my type.' Linda looked wistful for a moment before adding, 'I wished him well, of course. And I do hope he gets some professional help.'

The old lady patted her hand. 'Royally said, my dear. No need to settle for second best when there are so many more princes in the pond. '

Linda giggled. 'Oh, FG, you'll never guess what happened just before I went out.'

'Hm?'

'Before I went to the concert. The doorbell rang and it was that hunky builder with a big bunch of flowers.' She giggled again. 'He was more embarrassed than I was. He came round to say sorry.'

'Flowers? Builder? He probably got them from a petrol station. Those flowers will be wilted by tomorrow.' The old lady opened her purple ledger and rummaged in her big silver bag. 'I must get to work. There is much to do.' Linda got up to go, but FG called her back. 'So what exactly is your 'type', my dear?'

The following day Felicia's Souk was buzzing with customers. Linda chatted effortlessly and at length with all who came to browse and buy. She had a way of making each and every one feel special, so that FG was able to give her undivided attention to the very important task of finding a delicate fascinator in a most specific shade of sea green for a most exacting mother-of-the-bride-to-be. When she then produced a dainty antique lace veil set with co-ordinating seed pearls for the bride there wasn't a dry eye in the shop.

'Oh she looks so beautiful,' Linda sighed.

'And so will you, my dear,' FG added quietly at her shoulder. 'You too will make a beautiful bride.'

They skipped lunch to deal with the rush, and it was late afternoon before they were able to draw breath and sit down to a cup of tea in the freesia-scented office.

'You were right about those flowers.' Linda said as she reached for a garibaldi.

'Hm?' FG was busy writing.

'The ones Dave gave me. When I got home last night they weren't just wilted, they'd completely shrivelled up.'

'Dave?' The old lady snapped her ledger shut.

'The builder who saw me in the nude. I gave him a piece of my mind about those flowers.'

FG looked up sharply. 'You've seen the builder again?'

'I bumped into him. He's on a job just round the corner – that building society by the off licence. The one with all the scaffolding.' Linda gazed towards the door. 'He asked me out.'

'I hope you turned him down.'

'Well of course, after those manky flowers. But if he asks again I might say yes.'

Hard as amethysts, the old lady's eyes looked deep into the clear blue of the girl's. 'I think it best not to, my dear. Our sights are set a bit higher than a builder with a bunch of cut-price weeds.'

She reached into her silver bag and Linda thought she glimpsed something flickering in its depths. FG pulled out a shiny purple pen and opened her ledger. The shop bell rang and she waved the girl away with a dismissive flick of her hand.

Minutes later, Linda rushed back into the office out of breath and pink cheeked. 'Oh, FG. You'll never believe what's just happened.'

The old lady didn't look up. 'Something amazing?'

'Jake Hawkmore just asked me out!'

'Jake Hawkmore?' FG continued writing furiously.

'The entrepreneur. He's in all the magazines — *Now*, *Heat*, even *Hello!* Eligible Bachelor of the Year. The most gorgeous man on the planet!'

Linda pointed to a glossy magazine on FG's desk. The old lady peered at the cover. 'The Crown Prince of Commerce? The government's new Enterprise Czar?'

Linda nodded emphatically.

'I wonder,' FG mused, 'what such a man was doing in our little shop.'

'That's the most amazing thing.' Linda blushed. 'He saw me onstage at the concert and he tracked me down. He wants to take me out tomorrow night.'

'How exciting.' FG agreed, laying down her pen and closing the ledger. Somewhere outside there was a terrible grating and crashing noise that sounded like scaffolding collapsing.

Linda jumped. 'What was that?'

'Nothing of significance to us, my dear.' FG smiled, her good humour quite restored. 'Now, what are you going to wear tomorrow night?'

'He seemed so nice.' Linda sobbed into FG's lavender-scented handkerchief. 'He picked me up in his Aston Martin. We went to BeBe Mara. Only celebs go there, nothing below C list. Everyone was staring and taking our picture – my outfit was perfect. We had a fantastic dinner, and champagne. He was a great dancer, so good-looking. I thought we were getting on really well.' She sniffed. 'But he wasn't at all like they said in all those magazines. When I tried to say goodnight outside the flats, he wouldn't take no for an answer.' A new tide of sobs overcame the girl as she held up a mangled purple and silver sheath dress. 'I'm so sorry, FG. It's all ripped around the hem and the neck. I tried washing it, but I can't get the blood out.'

The old lady slumped in her chair, her violet eyes dimmed. 'Blood?' she whispered.

'His nose. I nutted him – and I got a few kicks in too. Then Dave arrived and finished him off.' Linda dried her eyes.

'Dave the builder?' FG's normally rosy cheeks sagged greyly. 'But he's... He couldn't have...'

'He was on his way home from the hospital. Remember that crash we heard yesterday? It was the scaffolding round the corner where Dave's been working. He was so lucky, it should have been him up there, but he'd gone to the florist to ask for a refund. His mate nearly died, Dave's been sitting with him all hours.' Linda blew her nose and managed a little smile. 'The hospital's round the corner from my flat. Dave was just walking past when Jake got nasty. He was amazing!' Linda sighed, then added. 'Are you OK, FG? You look dreadful.'

The old lady rested her silvery head in her hands. 'Perhaps,' she said faintly, 'you would put the kettle on, my dear. I feel a little unwell.'

'I'll open a window. It's a bit stale in here today.'

As Linda was making tea and opening a packet of digestives, the shop bell jangled. Hearing muffled voices FG pulled herself out of her chair and opened the office door a little wider, leaning on the handle for support.

She heard Linda's voice, playful and girlish. 'I hoped you'd call in.'

Then a deeper, rougher reply, 'I wanted to make sure you were OK, pet. How did it go with the police?'

'They were fine. Did they give you a hard time?'

'Nah, sounds like he's got form – and he wants it kept quiet. Well, I'd best get back to the site. Health and Safety want to see me about the accident – down side of being the boss. Are we still on for tonight?'

'If you promise not to pounce on me.'

'I wouldn't dare, pet. I've seen you in action.'

'Hang on a minute. Before you go, I want you to meet FG.'

FELICIA'S SOUK

'Who's FG?'

'She owns the shop. FG's short for Felicia Gildenfleur – she says that's too much of a mouthful. But I think it's short for Fairy Godmother too. That's what she's been to me.'

'I don't believe in fairies.'

FG clutched at her heart.

In the middle of the day, in the middle of the city, in the middle of a park, on a weathered wooden bench, a pretty girl was crying. She was mostly dressed in black. Her shoes, her stockings, her dress were all black, and her long golden plait was tied with a black ribbon. The man holding her hand was also dressed in black, his broad shoulders squeezed into a jacket designed for a less developed physique.

'She was such a special person.' The girl with the black bow sniffed between sobs. 'I only knew her a few weeks, but she was almost like family. She was so kind to me.'

'What'll you do now?' the man in the black suit asked as he wiped her tears away.

'Well, I'll have to find another job.'

'Marry me instead, pet. My family owns Kings Premier Properties – we're loaded. I'll buy you that souk shop if you want. Though I think you should set your sights a bit higher.'

Belvedere Road

Well, of course the whole thing was perfect. What else would you expect with Fiona at the helm? In her sea-green silk mother-of-the-bride number and co-ordinating fascinator – probably from one of those expensive boutiques in the old town. Doesn't look a day over forty-five and she must be well into her fifties by now. Wrinkles are simply forbidden in Fiona's world.

    The church was very old, fourteenth century I believe. Very few weddings are performed there, but of course the vicar was happy to oblige. Quite a plain building, but the stained glass windows were exquisite in the sunshine. With the floral arrangements, and the ladies in their colourful outfits, everything looked divine. Expensive with not a hint of the ostentatious. Precisely the note Fiona would strike.

I had a good look round at what everyone was wearing. Mainly those floaty, floral outfits that are so in vogue. And any number of hats – a few of them rather ill-considered. Particularly the mother-of-the-groom, but perhaps the enormous brim was intended as camouflage rather than style. Better not to risk comparison with Fiona. A faded blonde perm couldn't measure up to her glossy chestnut bob. Grey hairs are also forbidden in Fiona's world.

Of course a wedding is a chance for the ladies to shine – the gentlemen should blend into the background like the churchyard. Well, it seems the man next to me had a different opinion. His suit was sober enough, I suppose, but as for his tie ... bright green. And the pattern was most inappropriate for a place of worship – or anywhere else. I wouldn't have sat there only the church was packed and all the good seats were reserved for Fiona's inner circle. So I ended up next to that scruffy little goblin of a man. Mid-sixties, going to seed, and reeking of cigarettes. Thank heavens for the scent of those flowers. He tried to catch my eye as I sat down, so I left a decent gap between us and pretended not to notice. Which, let me tell you, was very difficult with him fidgeting about with his lighter the whole time.

It was a beautiful day, of course. Not a cloud in the sky, Fiona would never have allowed it. But it was quite draughty at the back of that church. I wished the bride would hurry up so we could get out in the sunshine again. Then I noticed people were mumbling in those hushed voices they use in the presence of God. But I wasn't close enough to join in, and I certainly didn't want to strike up a conversation with Mr Green Tie. I could tell what it was about, though, because people were starting to look at their watches, and then at the door. Where was the bride? An anxious moment for the family, all that planning and preparation and money spent, but where was Victoria? Well, I was quite worried for poor Fiona. How awful it would be if the bride didn't show up.

As if that woman's daughter would put a foot wrong. Precious wee Victoria had been nurtured and cosseted towards this shining moment from an early age, no time, expense or maternal attention spared. She made her entrance just before the mumbling turned to muttering. Late enough for a frisson of nervous excitement, but not a tasteless outburst of panic. Of course I didn't have a very good view from my draughty little corner at the back of the church, but I managed a glimpse of the bride in her designer dress with a vintage ivory lace veil – complete with little seed pearls to match Fiona's outfit. Like a haute couture fairy princess. And the entourage: pretty bridesmaids (not too pretty, of course); sweet little flower girl and pageboy (surprisingly well behaved); and the father of the bride puffed out with pride. Oh yes, Rupert was just as handsome as I remembered, tall and stately, that thick, dark hair of his turned to a most distinguished silver. How all the girls in our set grieved the day he announced he was marrying Fiona, a girl nobody had even heard of.

The walk up the aisle was perfectly choreographed, of course, not a foot or a chord out of place – that girl certainly takes after her mother. Then Rupert took his position next to Fiona. You could see he was still in her thrall, even after all these years, from the proprietorial way he tucked her hand over his arm. But oddly, at this climax of her maternal schemes, Fiona was gazing off into the distance as though her thoughts were somewhere else. Somewhere far away.

December 1980
The low winter sun was streaming in too brightly through the shop window, highlighting the corners the cleaner had missed. The blinds still hadn't arrived; it would take an extra two weeks to match the exact grey of the new furniture. Fiona wiped a duster across the counter and strategically placed a vase of lilies to mask the smell of the overflowing ashtray Mike had balanced on top of a precarious pile of files and manuals. She watched him squinting at the screen as he bashed frantically at the keyboard – the oil men were due in ten minutes. A sudden slip of his fingers, a curse and the cigarette fell from his lips. Mike darted to the rescue of his new carpet – a

microsecond too late. Fiona sighed as he wedged the cigarette back between his teeth and edged his chair over the scorch mark.

The murmur of the traffic on Belvedere Road was white noise and they both jumped as the outside door opened. Please, don't let it be the oil men – Fiona could see Mike wasn't ready. But it was only a couple of teenage lads come to browse the books and pretend they could afford the latest Commodore PET – 16K of memory, quite a step up from the 4K model Mike had been flogging from his spare room just a couple of years ago. The birth of home computing, that was what the press was calling it. Not enough of a money-spinner to fund the new showroom, though. That would take a big juicy order from the oil men. Cromemco – what Mike called 'the sexy stuff' – that was the future, the real processing power: a full 32K with dual eight inch floppies, and the promise of an upgrade to a hard disk in twelve months.

The teenaged lads were hovering around the books. Sometimes Mike was generous with his time, and his out-of-date magazines or samples. But today he was unusually focussed.

'Fiona,' he hissed under his breath, 'get rid of them before the real customers get here!'

Fiona was happy for an excuse to stay in the showroom, even the cloying scent of the lilies was better than the odour of ashtray, soldering iron and damp carpet that lurked in the cramped office out the back. She leant against the counter, her lovely long legs crossed at the ankles, and answered a couple of questions about the PET. The teenagers' tongues were all but hanging out: the fat one for the micro-computer, the spotty one for Fiona.

'Anything else, lads?' Fiona didn't wait for them to answer. 'We're closing early for lunch today. Why don't you take a brochure?'

Then she rounded them out onto the street, treating the spotty one to a charming smile as she shut the door in his face.

'D'you finish that memory board?' Mike didn't even look up.

'Very funny, Mike. Soldering is not in my job description. You're cheap enough to buy in kits as an economy drive, you break your own nails on them.'

Fiona paused for another breath of lilies and spotted two sharply dressed men climbing out of a taxi in the street outside.

'They're here.' She opened the door.

'Shit! Shit! Shit!!' The computer beeped a response. Mike dropped his cigarette again, stooped and came up smiling, oblivious to the ash now speckling his ginger beard.

'Gentlemen! Right on time. Come on in. Sh...Sit down. How was your journey? Fiona – get the coffee on, love!'

Fiona took the oil men's coats. Then she swept through the rear office and out of the back door to the little kitchenette and toilet they shared with the Christian Scientist Reading room.

A lengthy hour later, Fiona watched the three suits turn the corner onto the High Street. Mike, the short scruffy one in the middle, was taking the oil men to *Chillies* for lunch, hoping to impress them into a deal. He'd be in a foul mood later – they weren't going to bite.

Letting out a slow breath, Fiona locked the front door, and turned the Open sign to Closed. She tidied away the sales lit and manuals, emptied the still smouldering ashtray, and shut down the Cromemco. Christmas shopping or lunch? Lunch. She was in no mood for crowds. Fiona tried to find a comfortable position on the new electric-blue sofa, a triumph of style over function. The coffee table was slightly too low for ergonomic comfort, but she arranged a ham salad roll, a can of orangeade and a magazine in a neat geometric pattern on its smooth grey surface. Lady Diana Spencer smiled shyly up at her from the magazine's cover and Fiona permitted herself a short daydream about marrying the future King of England. But she didn't open the magazine, or even pick up her sandwich. There was much to think about and a rare quiet time to do so.

Much to think about indeed. Rupert, her fiancé, the love of her life. The man she was marrying in the spring. The future father of her children ... except that last night he had made it absolutely clear there would be no children. Fiona, who had spent her childhood nurturing an extended family of baby dolls, was left in shock, struggling to understand. Granted, Rupert's career was embryonic. For the foreseeable future they would need Fiona's salary, such as it was. She could understand now was not the time. In a few years, then? When his career was established? When they were settled in a nice house, with a garden? Rupert was adamant – no children.

Fiona had tried again. Yes, his job in the diplomatic service would mean moving abroad, perhaps even between different countries. Other families managed. The expat life would be broadening for their children. For their child? And they could always consider boarding school later, when educational stability became important. But no. Rupert wouldn't budge.

OK then. True, Rupert's father was indifferent to Rupert and his siblings, and his mother was a self-centred pleasure-seeker with no interest in her offspring. Rupert and Fiona would be different. They would go to all the classes, antenatal and post. Read Penelope Leach and every other expert in print. They would love their child. But Rupert was immovable and Fiona, who had never before needed to ask him twice for anything, ran out of words. A life without children? Or a life without Rupert? There were plenty of girls eager to take her place, all of whom would be considered far more suitable than Fiona: Posh Patricia, Horsey Harriet … And Nasty Nina right at the head of the queue. Oh yes, there was much for Fiona to think about.

She patted her eyes dry to preserve her makeup. Reaching for the orangeade she looked up to see faces at the window. Oh for heaven's sake – the two lads were back. They tapped on the window and gesticulated towards the door. Fiona flashed a brief smile and pointed to the Closed sign. But they didn't go away. So she took her lunch into the dark of the back room.

This was the room the clients never saw, crammed with ill-fitting second hand furniture. Two desks faced each other in the centre, little available surface on either. An oversized, and already outmoded, electric typewriter took up most of Fiona's desk, the stationery, letter-trays, and papers arranged with spatial perfection around the edges. Fiona was too unsettled to work, too churned-up to eat. She needed a distraction to retrieve her from the brink of a life-changing decision, so she looked across at Mike's desk.

It was an ever-shifting landscape of paperwork, manuals and text books populated by half-finished cups of coffee, Mike's beloved Beatles cassettes, packets of resistors or capacitors, and the odd girlie mag. Time for a tidy up. Besides which, the executive swivel chair was preferable to Fiona's budget secretarial model, so she brushed off the crumbs and ash, sank into its dubious comfort and turned on the radio.

BELVEDERE ROAD

'... so here's the Fab Four with *Christ You Know It Ain't Easy* ...'

Fiona fully agreed with the sentiment. She had nothing against the Mersey sound, but Mike had been playing his favourite band all morning. More a Roxy Music or Police fan herself, she fiddled with the dial.

'... that haunting Lennon and McCartney classic – *Yesterday* ...'

Oh for goodness sake. Fiona tried another station, tuning in to the clashing, closing notes of *A Day in the Life*. She closed her eyes and waited for the next song. *Imagine* – what was going on? It must be a Beatle's birthday or something. Still, Fiona quite liked this one. She hummed along as she stacked Mike's cassettes in alphabetical order.

'That was the late great John Lennon. Gunned down last night outside his New York apartment. Rest in peace, John, we love you.'

Thankful for the safe, hands-off grief of a public tragedy, Fiona cried.

It was almost dark by the time Mike returned. From her post at the window, Fiona watched him shamble along Belvedere Road. As she could have predicted, he was drunk, defeated, and defensive with it.

'Why's the sodding Closed sign still up? Are you trying to lose me money? We're going to need all the book and game sales we can make.' Red in the face, he didn't notice how white Fiona's was.

'Come in the back, Mike. I'll make you a coffee.'

'I don't need a sodding coffee, you silly cow. I need a sodding contract.'

Fiona winced, but replied quietly, 'come in the back, Mike. You're drunk and it's bad for business.'

'It's my sodding business!' But he staggered obediently through to the office as Fiona locked the door.

She stood beside him and watched as he slumped in his executive chair. 'So what happened?'

'They let me buy lunch then told me they were going to sign with Gordon Halliday's mob instead. Bigger quantity discount.' Mike sunk his head in his hands.

Fiona looked down at the grey already showing through his ginger hair and thought he needed a good cut. 'We can't match it?'

'At that price I'd be paying them to take the kit away.' He banged his fist on the desk and a pile of files slid to the floor. Fiona replaced them in silence and went to make the coffee.

When she returned, Mike was smoking in the dark. She held out the mug and he took it. He offered a cigarette and she took that.

'Have you heard the news at all today, Mike?'

'When do I have time to listen to the sodding news?'

'There was some terrible news. A real shock.' Fiona chose her words carefully. 'John Lennon's been shot dead.'

BELVEDERE ROAD

For a long, long moment, Mike just stared at her. Then it was even worse than she had predicted, and she'd known it would be bad. He stood up. He dropped the coffee and the cigarette. Then he sat again, missed the chair and fell to the floor. Fiona put out her own cigarette and safely retrieved Mike's. She helped him up. She felt him shaking, heard his muttered broken 'No. Oh No. No. No.' She saw his blotched face wet with tears, his nose and moustache shiny with snot. A strange, almost maternal, tenderness made her put her arms around him. He smelt of booze and spicy food, cigarettes and aftershave. She ruffled his ginger hair and traced the line of his beard, deciding to book him in for a trim.

Mike's head shifted against Fiona's lovely breasts and he sighed. As her long, cool fingers stroked his hair, he nuzzled, tentatively at first. Then he slipped his arms round her waist and clung a little, just a little. It wasn't the first time her boss had tried it on, but this time Fiona thought, 'Oh, what the hell'. She held him a bit tighter. Mike went for it.

It wasn't comfortable. The landscape that was Mike's desk was rocky and treacherous and Fiona hit her head on the typewriter when she tried to shuffle to safety. It wasn't elegant. Speed of access was the priority – Mike's trousers stuck around his knees, Fiona's blouse and bra rolled up under her armpits. Nor was it tender or romantic – Mike's moustache tasted of cigarettes, red wine and Mexican food, and the zip on Fiona's skirt caught in his pubic hair. But what it was, despite all that, was suddenly, intensely, and mind-blowingly satisfying.

Eyes refocusing, hearts thumping, they pulled apart. Mike tripped and sat heavily on a box of memory board kits. Fiona manoeuvred herself delicately off the desk, pausing to peel the top sheet of the unsigned oil company contract off her bottom. They looked quickly at each other then looked quickly away.

Mike pulled himself and his trousers up and edged towards the door. 'I'll get some toilet paper.'

'Don't go down the hall, you'll scare the Christian Scientists.' Fiona laughed. 'There's a packet of tissues in my handbag. Front pocket. And, for goodness sake, give me another cigarette.'

They tidied themselves up. Fiona lolled in the executive chair enjoying the moment Mike became aware of the excruciating discomfort of the budget secretarial model. They finished their coffee, smoked cigarettes, and drank a bottle of single malt, an early Christmas offering from the furniture rep. Mike drunkenly shed more tears over John Lennon and his own lost youth. Fiona drunkenly sobbed over her ruined dreams.

'He'll come round.' Mike said.

'What if he doesn't?' Fiona scrubbed at her wasted mascara with the last of the tissues. 'What if I marry him, and I throw away my chance to have children.'

'I'd love kids. I've always wanted kids.'

'No you haven't, Mike. Anyway, I adore Rupert and I don't usually even fancy you.'

Mike laughed. 'I wasn't proposing. I couldn't leave Yvonne, especially at the moment. I need the old bag's money to prop up the business.' He glanced coyly at Fiona. 'No, you marry Rupert – he's a bit of a plonker, but he's a sound enough bloke. And you can't let Nasty Nina get her claws in. Still, if you ever do happen to fancy me again...'

'It won't happen again, Mike. Not ever. But I don't want that to spoil things here. I'd like to keep my job.' She looked him frankly in the face. 'Can we manage that? No funny comments or little asides?'

'Yes, love. We can manage that.' He grinned. 'It was good, though, wasn't it?'

Fiona smiled back. 'Fucking fantastic.'

Of course wedding photographers always take forever, and it's so dull for anyone who isn't family. First those endless photographs at the church, then we all trooped through a little gate and across some lawns to the reception and he started clicking away all over again. This family group and that, and this group of friends and that, then all the rest of us – those not important enough to be in any of the other groups. He took a lot of Fiona and Victoria together, with a little soft focus they'll look just like sisters, except Fiona's much taller. And Victoria's a red head, of course.

BELVEDERE ROAD

The reception was in the ballroom. It was a very grand affair, I dread to think of the cost. So many important people, but of course I didn't know most of them, and those I did were quite a distance away on the head table. I was seated near the door, with two elderly ladies who bickered throughout, and that scruffy man from the church who kept calling me Tina although I told him my name twice. Fortunately, there was also a very pleasant Australian couple at our table. And they had such a nugget of news. The happy couple were off to live in Sydney after the honeymoon! They had all the details: Greg had been headhunted to set up a new business venture, and Victoria's company had asked her to manage their Sydney IT department. Well, it was certainly news to me and the old ladies were very shocked. But Mr Green Tie didn't seem surprised at all. Everyone said what good luck it was for them both. Still, I wondered to myself, how will Fiona fill her time without Project Victoria?

The speeches were rather long. The groom's was as gushing as these things usually are, and the best man's as vulgar. But the father-of-the-bride put those younger men to shame. I'd forgotten what a handsome man Rupert was. Such authority, such sincerity – all too rare in a politician these days. It was a beautiful speech. He said he hoped the newly-weds would find all the happiness, companionship and trust he and Fiona had shared over the years. Then, and this was a really touching moment, he confessed that he'd initially had doubts about bringing a child into the world. But Fiona had persuaded him, and now their daughter, Victoria, was the apple of his eye and this moment was the crowning experience of his life. There was hardly a dry eye in the room. Especially when he proposed a toast to the happy couple and wished them well in their new life in Australia. I looked over at Fiona then, but there wasn't a flicker, just the same serene, self-satisfied smile.

After the speeches I sat with the Australians, chatting and watching the dancing. The newly-weds had their first waltz, then Fiona and Rupert joined them on the dance floor. Of course everyone said they made a charming couple, tall and elegant, a perfect match. I was able to fill them in on the early years and they were amazed at Fiona's humble beginnings. The whole affair went on very late, I thought the band would never stop playing and it wouldn't do to leave before the bride and groom. All very well for those with luxury rooms at the hotel of course, but I didn't relish the long trek back to my little B&B.

Then, at last, it was time to wave the happy couple off. The bride looked exquisite in her going-away outfit. Fiona and Rupert stood arm in arm on the steps of the hotel, and as the car pulled away I noticed a single tear on Fiona's cheek. She's always possessed such self-control, Patricia and Harriet used to say she was rather a cold fish. Anyway, it was getting very chilly and I just was about to go inside when I noticed something most peculiar.

Rupert went back to the reception, but Fiona stayed outside. I thought she might be feeling a bit blue, what with her only child off to live on the other side of the world and I was about to go over for a chat when she headed across the lawn. So I followed, at a discreet distance. Just to make sure she was alright.

And then I saw the man with the green tie. He was sitting on the grass smoking a cigarette. Fiona walked up and sat down next to him. Then she sort of curled up in a ball with her arms wrapped around her head and I could hear her sobbing. Just sobbing and sobbing there in the dark while the man with the green tie held her.

After a while she stopped crying and sat up a bit. Her fascinator was all squashed and askew. Mr Green Tie lit a cigarette and gave it to her. Well, I thought, that was very strange because I happen to know that Fiona's never been a smoker.

Then I looked at that scruffy goblin with the ginger hair, and I thought about elfin little Victoria standing next to Rupert and Fiona. And, just for a moment, everything seemed to fall into place. It was absurd, of course. Ridiculous and absurd – probably slanderous. But what if it was true? Perhaps Fiona wasn't perfect after all.

I wondered if I should go over, just to see if everything was alright. Well, she seemed so upset.

BELVEDERE ROAD

But I knew Fiona wouldn't want someone from the outer circle at a time like this. No, she would want her husband. So I went inside to find Rupert. I was sure *he'd* know what to do.

The Green Tie

It was his lucky tie. The one he wore for important meetings or hot dates. It didn't have a hundred percent success rate, more like nine and a quarter – not great, but way above Mike's average. Not that he had many important meetings these days. Or, for that matter, many hot dates.

The tie was silk, with a self-coloured pattern of a naked lady that you could only see when the light caught it a certain way. It was emerald green – not to everyone's taste apparently, though Mike couldn't see why. Women always did a double take when he wore the green tie. It was the sort of finishing touch that got you noticed.

THE GREEN TIE

His ex-secretary, the lovely Fiona, had given him the green tie as a going away present when Mike crossed the pond to Silicon Valley in the early eighties. 'I thought of you as soon as I saw it,' she said, handing him the *TieShop* package with a little smile. 'Think of me when you wear it.' And so every time he knotted the tie Mike obediently thought of Fiona and her perfect breasts.

Mike's wife, Yvonne, never liked his lucky tie. But then she never liked Fiona either, nor, for that matter, any of his female employees over the years – she seemed to think he was sleeping with them all. Despite Mike's general lack of success, Yvonne did have a point, because he would happily have bedded any one of them given encouragement. Plus, Mike's accent, though no great shakes in the South of England, was an instant babe magnet when they first arrived in California, bestowing a glamour that made up for him being short and scruffy with ginger hair and a poorly trimmed beard. And Mike found the green tie was a great icebreaker in all sorts of social situations.

Happy days, before the huge restaurant platters got to Mike's waistline and arteries. Before he branched out on the internet just as the dot-com bubble burst. And before Yvonne, who had already begun to resemble a creature from *Star Wars*, pursued her fascination with cosmetic surgery one disastrous step too far, dying on the operating table from liposuction complications.

THE GREEN TIE

Although the marriage had been one of convenience for them both, her death was a big shock to Mike. Yvonne had wanted a husband and didn't care that he was a randy little fox of a man with few social graces. Mike had needed someone to bankroll his business ventures and was happy to put up with a woman whose silhouette reminded him of the room-sized computers of his early career. Neither blessed nor cursed with offspring after three decades of marriage, the couple had little in common but the years they'd spent together. Still they'd muddled by. Mike played the obedient husband in public, while Yvonne's aptitude for investment financed a very comfortable LA lifestyle. She'd stuck by him through better and worse, through richer and poorer (at times considerably poorer on Mike's part). And when the clinic telephoned with the bad news, Mike realised he'd quite miss the old bag.

He decided on a low key send-off, Yvonne's friends weren't really his, and her many acquaintances were as scary as a wake of benevolent vultures. After the funeral Mike planned to visit the mother country. He'd look up a few old friends. Take in some old haunts. Play the tourist for a while. Leave it open-ended and see what came up. California was great, but he was suddenly homesick for rain and warm beer, and the old days.

The meeting with Yvonne's lawyer was just a formality, but it was still an occasion for Mike's lucky

THE GREEN TIE

green tie. After all, it's not every day a man gets a snapshot of how rich he's about to become. By the time he drove home again, he'd seen more than a mere snapshot. He had the full screen panoramic vista in glorious Technicolor.

Mike staggered to the poolside bar and picked up the nearest bottle of malt whisky. Cats? When had Yvonne become so interested in cats? He emptied a large crumpled envelope onto the bar, searching for a particular document, a particular passage: *'All our married life I wanted a cat, but you said you hated them. When it became apparent there would be no children, I asked again. You suggested a budgie.'* Mike lit a cigarette. Through his gathering Scotch mist, he vaguely remembered a brief exchange about pets. So all this was about a non-existent moggie? He scanned further down the page. *'It's the cats' turn now, Mike. You and your scams have had your last handout.'* That really stung. Schemes, maybe. Scams, never!

He reached for a crystal tumbler, noticing for the first time the etched Siamese cats dancing around the base. With newly focussed eyes, Mike saw the matching ice-bucket and the tabbies in sunglasses appliquéd on the poolside cushions. A quick tour of the ground floor netted mugs, plates, lamps, coasters, and several litters of figurines. He piled them onto a fluffy white rug (complete with ears and tail) and dragged the lot outside.

Mike lined the larger cats along the edge of the pool, retaining the smaller ornaments to use as missiles. He slumped on a lounger, swigging scotch from the bottle – the crystal tumblers had already found a watery grave. Stubbing his cigarette out on Yvonne's favourite statuette (a sizable lump of alabaster, some Egyptian feline he assumed), Mike took a few pot shots as he pondered his future: the forthcoming spectacle of his own financial ruin. Maybe he could sell Yvonne's corpse for cat meat.

The scotch made him sweat, and he loosened his tie. Lucky tie? Might as well hang himself with it. Mike considered the practicalities. The diving board? The balcony outside the master bedroom? There was a fair drop from the gallery in the reception hall. As he rolled off the lounger to investigate possible suicide sites, his phone rang. Mike snatched it up snarling, 'Forget it do-gooder. The cats got the lot.'

'Indeed?' a cultured English voice replied. 'I'd never have had you pegged as a cat-lover.'

Mike could hear her smiling from all the way across the Atlantic. He smiled back, stretching out on the lounger and kicking off his shoes.

'Fiona, love! You got my email? How the hell are you? And our beautiful Vicky? What about your plonker of a husband? I'm wearing your tie.' Mike lit another cigarette. 'Oh, I'm up shit creek, love. And no sodding paddle!' One last swallow of scotch. 'Nah, you know me. I'll bounce back. I'm better off without the old boot.' He lobbed the empty bottle at the pool, adding a two-fingered farewell as a lamp and a couple of mugs took a dive. 'Course I'll be at the wedding – 'bout time I visited the old home land.'

The phone call cheered Mike up a bit. He retrieved the scattered papers from the bar, dispatching a few more cats en route. The net result of his wife's will was this: an unspecified provision for the funeral; a generous bequest to an elderly Aunt Winifred, Yvonne's sole remaining blood relation back in the UK; and the remainder, the lion's share, to the cats. Nothing for Mike. Yet he suddenly grinned.

Mike determined to say goodbye to his wife in style. Blow the expense, one last thrash before the cats got their claws in. Yvonne would have a film star's send off. He selected a fifty thousand dollar funeral package, followed by a finger buffet for three hundred guests at the Beverley Hills Balmoral Hotel. Since their arrival Stateside a quarter of a century ago, Yvonne had built up a considerable database of acquaintances. She ensured their loyalty with regular and generous donations to carefully selected causes, monitoring the charities industry over the years to stay on trend. Whatever these acquaintances might say about Yvonne in private, Mike reckoned the lure of the Balmoral, plus the opportunity to canvass her widower, should be enough to guarantee a good turnout.

The funeral was great fun. Mike wore his green tie, telling everyone it was Yvonne's favourite. Somehow he maintained his doleful expression as the pallbearers struggled under the weight of the coffin, unaware it was stuffed with thousands of dollars worth of cat merchandise. He gave a spirited and colourful tribute, and, if the assembled society found the sentiments inappropriate, they put it down to a combination of grief and British eccentricity.

The sympathetic hugs were very enjoyable, as was the limousine back to the hotel. Mike had a right laugh at the do, swigging champagne and promising donations to all those snooty skinny birds in black hats. And the networking opportunities were fantastic – he made some very tasty contacts and even found a couple of potential backers for his Satellite Palmtop *'For when you're climbing that mountain and Wi-Fi just can't cut it'*. The tie was working its magic, news of his financial ruin hadn't got out yet. With any luck he'd make it out of the country before the shit hit the fan. If he managed to get a handshake from one of the Californians before he left, the shit might never hit at all.

Taking a break from the millionaires, Mike stepped outside for a cigarette and gazed up at a plane high in the blue. Back at the house a large ostrich-leather suitcase was waiting, packed with the cream of his walk-in closet. Beside it, a one way ticket to Heathrow and his Gucci carry-on containing in-flight essentials: laptop, thriller, toothbrush, condoms – though he always kept one in his wallet as well. You never knew your luck.

THE GREEN TIE

Mike headed back to the party for a final schmooze. Over by the buffet he spotted a middle-aged woman in a feathery black hat and one of those funny little woollies that didn't do up properly but made her boobs stick out a treat. She was all alone. She smiled at him sympathetically. Mike checked his watch: at least a couple of hours before he needed to leave for the airport. He patted his wallet and straightened his lucky green tie.

The Spoiler of the Fun

Jessica opened the door of the holiday cottage and stepped out into the bright August morning, pausing for a restorative breath of air. She allowed herself a moment to be soothed by the familiar surroundings: the meadow, wild with untamed grasses and pretty with delicate flowers; the downs in the distance, rising green and gentle against the blue sky; the tree-lined path that led up to the cliff then down through leafy tunnels to the beach below. A small corner of her world untouched by thirty years of real life.

Pulling herself back to the demands of the now, Jessica made a mental checklist of the paraphernalia she would need for the day ahead: drinks, snacks, tissues, wet wipes, port-a-potty, camera, change for

THE SPOILER OF THE FUN

the car park, discounted-entry vouchers. She looked down at her comfortable low-heeled pumps and hardwearing neutrals – essential wear for a day out with the family. She looked up at the sky – a few clouds out at sea, better take waterproofs for everyone. Another breath, then back into the cottage and back into the fray.

'Chloe! Lewis! Shoes on. We want to get there before the crowds and I need to allow an extra half hour to collect Gran and Auntie Winn from the hotel.'

Three-year-old Lewis crawled out from under the sofa with an armful of dinosaurs, bright blue eyes matching bright blue striped top – blue and white stripes, easy to spot in the crowds when he ran off later.

'Just one dinosaur, Lewis.'

Eight-year-old Chloe appeared from the bedroom, blonde plaits, pretty-in-pink – bright pink, also easy to spot.

'I wish Daddy was here instead of Auntie Winn. She smells funny.'

I wish he was here too, thought Jessica, smoothing her short brown hair in the mirror and absentmindedly reapplying her lipstick. 'That's perfume, Chloe. And Daddy has to be in Beijing this week. Shoes, children. Now! We're running late.' She gathered up the waterproofs, 'I said just one dinosaur, Lewis! Come on. Out to the car. Fantasy Chine today.'

THE SPOILER OF THE FUN

The hotel was a mere twenty minutes walk along the cliff path. But by road it was five miles inland and out again along narrow country lanes that fell steeply as they neared the coast. Jessica hated that drive, she was liable to meet a coach-load of tourists at any moment and somehow she always ended up with the tricky manoeuvring. Focussing on the road, she tried to close her mind to the children's chatter.

'Mummy, why does Auntie Winn have to come on holiday with us?' Chloe's voice broke her concentration.

'Because Gran wants her friend to come on holiday too,' Jessica replied automatically.

'But Auntie Winn says she doesn't like the Isle of Wight, and if she wasn't here then Gran could stay in the cottage like she usually does.'

Jessica continued her daughter's train of thought without speaking. Yes, and I wouldn't have to do this stupid drive four times a day. And I wouldn't have to bite my tongue twenty times a day. And I wouldn't have to hear a hundred times a day 'It's alright, Lorna. I'm sure Jessica knows best.'

She stopped herself and got her thoughts in order. Today was going to be a lovely day. She had carefully selected Fantasy Chine and it was perfect for everyone with large fibreglass creatures and adventure playgrounds for Chloe and Lewis plus pretty gardens and craft barns for Auntie Winn and Gran. Jessica was determined that everyone would have a wonderful time.

THE SPOILER OF THE FUN

At the Beachcomber Hotel, they had to wait for Auntie Winn to have words with the manager about the previous night's dinner, fetch her umbrella from the room and then make one last trip to the loo. By which time, Chloe had to be prised away from the giant hotel TV, while Lewis had streaked chocolate caramel all over his blue and white stripes. 'Just a little treat, dear.' Auntie Winn smiled. 'You're so strict with them.'

Auntie Winn's fulsome, matronly figure and matching voice dominated the family car, even smothering the sound of the children singing along with Gran in the back. The journey that would have taken fifteen minutes if they'd gone straight from the cottage stretched to two hours, and Jessica's heart sank as they were corralled into a distant corner of the Fantasy Chine car park. Her heart sank further as they shuffled with the rest of the crowd to join the queues at the entrance. Then it plummeted as she realised the discounted entry vouchers were back in the car and she'd have to pay full price for three adults and two children. As they finally emerged into the sunlight, Lewis squealed 'Dinosaurs!' and made a run for it, just as Aunty Winn proclaimed, 'Time for lunch now. Don't you agree, Jessica?'

She forked out for lunch in the cafe, although there was nothing Lewis would touch. Auntie Winn wasn't keen on picnics, 'Why would anyone want to sit on damp grass, eating cheese and pickle baps, when there's a perfectly nice cafe with hot Cornish

THE SPOILER OF THE FUN

pasties and cream cakes?' After lunch they pottered round the craft barn where Lewis, deprived of dinosaurs, set about creating his own primeval forest among baskets of overpriced dried flowers.

When at last they set off around the park, Auntie Winn walked very slowly, making a fuss every time the path turned up or down hill. Gran hung back keeping her company. Feeling out of pocket and out of sorts, Jessica tried to keep the children from running on ahead. She felt like a sheep dog dashing backwards and forwards along paths lined with fibreglass dinosaurs, grinning pirates and jungle animals. Jessica tried to keep it jolly, but by mid afternoon everyone had felt the frayed edge of her temper, the children most of all.

'Bloody woman,' Jessica muttered to herself, surreptitiously giving Auntie Winn the evil eye. It wasn't just the trip to Fantasy Chine, the bloody woman was ruining the whole holiday. And it should have been so perfect, like it used to be back in Jessica's childhood. That was why she brought her family to the island year after year; she was laying down perfect memories for her own children. But this year everything was going wrong.

First Henry had to go to Beijing on urgent business, though how could any business be urgent enough to interfere with your family's summer holiday? They'd had a terrible row and the atmosphere lingered until he left for the airport. Then Jessica's mother announced her friend was

THE SPOILER OF THE FUN

coming too and they would stay together at the Beachcomber Hotel instead of at the cottage. Auntie Winn had come into a bit of money from some niece who'd dropped dead over in America, so she was treating them both to a week of luxury instead of 'roughing it' with the children. Auntie Winn wasn't even a real auntie, just an interfering friend who'd had an opinion on everything Jessica had said and done since puberty.

A childhood phrase came to her mind: The Spoiler of the Fun. That was Auntie Winn alright. Even without Henry everything would have been fine if her mother had been at the cottage with them. If they hadn't had to crawl everywhere at a snail's pace. If they hadn't had to accommodate Auntie bloody Winn all the bloody time.

They climbed up the hill to Cowboy Town. Jessica parked the two old ladies on a bench while she wore herself out chasing the children in and out of the Wild West buildings, firing cap guns and dodging the other tourists. Doing all the things Henry would do if he'd been with his family instead of with his job. After a breathless but happy half hour, they returned to the bench. Gran and Auntie Winn had gone.

Jessica grabbed a child in each hand and dragged them back round Cowboy Town, in and out of the saloon, the jail, the Wells Fargo office. Back down the hill. Round and round the maze of paths. Past jungle animals, pirates, grinning dinosaurs. Searching and searching for the old ladies. Backwards and forwards till Lewis was in tears and begging to be carried.

'I need the loo, Mummy.' Chloe pleaded quietly.

'Why didn't you go after lunch?' Jessica hauled her children over to the queue for the Ladies, still scanning the throngs of holidaymakers. Among the noisy, happy families, her gaze fixed on a small boy aged somewhere between her own children's ages. He was hiding with his mum behind the wooden fort, both wearing pirate headscarves and eye patches, fingers pressed to lips, stifling giggles as a baffled dad passed by looking for them. Why can't I be that sort of mother? Jessica thought bitterly. The sort of mother who has fun with her children, who makes them giggle not cry.

'Maybe Gran and Auntie Winn have been hiding?' Chloe whispered pulling at her mother's arm.

'Hm?'

'Look, Mummy.' She pointed to the cafe.

Two elderly ladies waved from the window, holding up plates of cakes.

'I simply don't see what all the fuss is about, Jessica. I was tired and I needed a cup of tea.' Wedged in a deckchair on the grass outside the holiday cottage, Auntie Winn was unrepentant.

'Well no, you never see do you? You never see further than your own needs and opinions.'

THE SPOILER OF THE FUN

'Jess! That's enough. You are going too far.' Her mother's voice sounded thinned and tired.

'Oh, I'd like to go much further, Mum, but the children are upset enough for one day.'

Across the meadow Lewis was chasing bubbles blown by his big sister. Chloe gave occasional glances back to the cottage and the grown-ups, checking to see if it was safe to return. Jessica waved to the children. 'Tea in fifteen minutes!' she called, forcing her shoulders down and her body into a more relaxed shape.

'We can't all tear about the place like you and the children, Jessica.' Auntie Winn insisted. 'Some of us are getting on a bit.'

'Then you didn't have to come along, did you? You could have had a nice quiet day at the hotel and Mum could have come without you.' Jessica could feel her mother's disapproval, her disappointment, but she carried on anyway. 'Perhaps you should do that tomorrow, have a day off from us.'

'Jess! Please stop this. I wanted Winn to come with me. And, besides, it's...'

'It's alright, Lorna,' Auntie Winn interrupted quickly. 'It must have been very stressful for Jessica with everyone to look after. We're all tired and upset and we need our tea. I'll go and see how that pie's doing.' She heaved herself out of the chair and into the cottage.

Jessica stared across the meadow to where the children were squabbling over the bubble mix. She

THE SPOILER OF THE FUN

knew her mother was upset and determined not to look at her in case there were tears. What sort of daughter was she? What sort of mother and daughter to make the people she loved so unhappy? A fine holiday she was giving them. The Spoiler of the Fun wasn't Auntie Winn after all.

Chloe held the bubble mix high above her head as Lewis kicked at her ankles, but Jessica hadn't the energy to intervene. She knew she should go and help Auntie Winn with the tea, but didn't trust herself to be in the same room. She knew she should apologise, but she wasn't going to. Instead she sat next to her mother, gaze fixed on the meadow.

Auntie Winn was calling from the cottage doorway, but nobody replied. She called again. 'Lorna? Cup of tea, dear?'

Jessica looked round. The bloody woman was so big she filled the doorway, no wonder she couldn't walk far. That was what a diet of pasties and cream cakes did for you.

'Lorna, dear? Have you dropped off?'

Auntie Winn moved so quickly that Jessica was still staring at the doorway when she realised her mother wasn't moving at all.

'You mustn't blame yourself, dear. You didn't know.' Auntie Winn and Jessica sat side by side, hand in hand, squashed together on the little sofa. Chloe and Lewis were asleep at last, dreaming bewildered

THE SPOILER OF THE FUN

dreams about Gran and the paramedics and the ambulance that had finally taken her away.

'I should have gone with her.' Jessica's voice was a husky, cried-out whisper.

'Oh, my dear child. We can't do anything for her now.' Auntie Winn stroked her hair, her body curved comfortingly around the girl she'd held as a baby. 'Why don't you try to sleep? I'll sit up in case the children wake.'

'She didn't tell me, Auntie Winn. Why didn't she tell me? I'd never have hauled her all over Fantasy Chine. I'd never have had that row. How could she be so irresponsible?' Jessica pushed the older woman away, voice rising as she rose to her feet.

'Oh, my dear. She didn't want you to know. She thought you wouldn't let her come, and she wanted this last holiday with you all so much. Your mum thought if we stayed at the hotel she could get plenty of rest and she'd be alright. She was going to tell you after the holiday.' Auntie Winn took Jessica's hand and sat her down again. 'You should rest, dear. There will be lots to do in the morning.'

'I need to go over to the hospital first thing. Will you stay here with the children, Auntie?'

'Of course. We'll walk down to the beach, have an ice-cream at the hotel ...' she paused, '... if that's alright with you, Jessica.'

'I'm sorry. I'm so sorry about everything. Of course they can have ice-cream. I wish we could start the holiday again, I wish I'd never said those things.

THE SPOILER OF THE FUN

Oh, Auntie Winn, I just wish I'd known.' She gasped, 'I never said goodbye.'

They held each other awkwardly on the little sofa. Both women crying again.

'I know, Jessica. I tried to get her to tell you, but she didn't want to spoil the holiday.'

'No, I did that. I'm the Spoiler of the Fun.'

Auntie Winn smiled a sad smile. 'That's what Lorna used to call herself. You're too hard on yourself, my dear, just like she was. A little family row or two — that's what holidays are about. Lorna was just happy to be here with you all. We both were.'

Jessica sniffed and reached for the last tissue. 'You go to bed, Auntie Winn. I couldn't sleep. It's almost dawn. I'll walk up the hill. Try to get a signal and call Henry. See if he managed to book a flight.'

'I'll make a cup of tea for when you get back. Then I think I will get my head down for a bit.' Auntie Winn's big voice seemed smaller. 'I do feel rather wrung out.'

Wrapped in a blanket, for comfort as much as warmth, Jessica hiked up to the cliff top and turned on her mobile phone to find a text from Henry: he'd be landing early evening and should be at the cottage that night. She walked slowly back across the meadow, in no hurry to return, no hurry to go anywhere. Her earlier shock was wearing off leaving behind a shivering nausea at the lack of sleep, lack of food, and lack of her mother.

THE SPOILER OF THE FUN

In the half light, Jessica saw a mug of tea and plate of biscuits waiting beside the deckchair. She wrapped her hand around the mug and smiled as she examined the biscuits – thick with chocolate and filled with flavoured cream, Auntie Winn could always be counted on for luxury goodies. She remembered her own mother complaining about the over-rich treats Jessica had loved as a child. Exasperating and inspiring in equal measures, Auntie Winn had been such a constant in her childhood, she took her love for granted. It was Auntie Winn who kept them all on course when Jessica's father died, who helped out with babysitting, homework, birthday parties, even Jessica's wedding. Auntie Winn, whose last known relative had passed away thousands of miles across the sea in America, whose lifelong best friend had died just hours ago. Auntie Winn who never complained about being lonely, but who would now be far more alone than Jessica could imagine.

'It's alright, Mum,' she said quietly. 'We'll look after her.'

The tea was getting cold, but Jessica nibbled her way through the biscuits. Nausea abating, she looked out across the meadow dazzled by the sunrise. To where, up on the cliff top, her mother, light as the mother of her youth, blew a kiss, then disappeared into the tunnel of green on her way down to the sea.

A Game of Pirates

Robert was having a fabulous day at Fantasy Chine. They'd been first in the queue for the water slides – him and Mum in one boat, racing Dad in the next. Dad got a wet bum, but he soon dried off in the sunshine. Then they had ice-creams. Dad said it was too early in the day, but Mum said they'd had an early start and they deserved a treat. And Mum and Dad didn't argue. They hadn't argued much all holiday, at least not in front of Robert.

This was much better than the holidays he usually went on. The ferry trip was great – loads more fun than waiting around at airports – and they'd been to the beach and the zoo and a farm, and had ice-cream every day. Fantasy Chine was Robert's own idea – it was on top of some brochures Mum gave him. There were lots of colourful pictures of families laughing and playing together and Robert knew it would be brilliant. He skipped along holding hands with Mum and Dad, and thought this might possibly be the happiest day of his life – all six and a half years of it.

Cowboy Town was his best bit. Dad bought Stetsons and cap guns which smelt burny and brilliant. Dad was the sheriff and Robert was his deputy. Mum held up the bank and they all had a gunfight in the dusty street and took photos of each other on the gallows. Dad lifted Robert up to sit on a big horse. It was massive, much higher than a real one. He lifted Mum up too. Dad was so big and strong, like a big, dark, hairy bear – especially when he got cross. Mum was so little and her hair was like sunshine – like a princess, except for her checked shirt and jeans. She wanted to stand up on the horse's back, but Robert was glad when Dad told her, 'Sit down. It's too slippery.'

Up on that horse Robert could see everything, all across Fantasy Chine and out to sea. Mum wrapped her arms around him and rested her head on his blonde curls. Dad smiled up at them both and took a photo. Yes, this really was the happiest day of his life.

Then Mum looked at her watch and said, 'Shit!'

Dad looked up. 'What's the matter?'

'I've left my pills in the car. I'm supposed to take one at eleven.' She shook her head. 'Nah, it'll be fine.'

A GAME OF PIRATES

Robert looked at Dad. 'You'd better not skip one, Mum.'

Mum smiled her brightest smile. 'I'll take two later. I'm not traipsing all the way back to the car for one little pill.'

Dad lifted them down from the horse. 'I'll go. Where are they, Luce?'

Mum said they were in the boot. She kissed Dad's cheek and called him her gallant knight. Dad raised his eyebrows and said he'd meet them at the dinosaurs. Then he set off at a jog down a wooded path signed 'Main Gate'.

'We'll be by the styracosaurus!' Mum called after him.

Robert thought for a moment. 'There isn't a styracosaurus, Mum.'

'Oh,' said Mum, 'I must have meant the triceratops.' She picked up her rucksack. 'Let's play a game.'

'What game?'

'A game of pirates! Come on, Lysander.'

'Mu-um,' Robert smiled and shook his finger at her, 'my name's Robert.'

'Only because Dad got to the registry office first,' Mum sang, rolling up her shirt sleeve. 'What does my tattoo say?'

Robert sighed, but his smile widened, 'Lysander my Love.'

'Right. So come on, Lysander. First stop – the Smugglers' Cave!'

A GAME OF PIRATES

They ran off down a different path and into the dark of the Smugglers' Cave. In a damp, rather smelly corner, away from the other holiday makers, Mum opened her rucksack and pulled out headscarves, eye-patches and a dark wig. Underneath her shirt she was wearing a stripy t-shirt, and there was one for Robert too. She stashed the cowboy hats, guns, and spare clothes in a plastic bag. By the time they came back out into the sunshine, the transformation was complete.

'Just like *Pirates of the Caribbean*,' Mum said. 'Look, I'm Jack Sparrow!'

Robert remembered watching a scary film, curled up on Mum's sofa with a big bowl of popcorn. 'My cowboy hat!' He turned back.

'Later, me hearty. Come on!' Mum took hold of his hand and they set off again at a run.

They nearly bumped into Dad by the cafe, but Mum pushed Robert behind the Pirate Fort, and they crouched down, fingers pressed to their lips, stifling giggles. Dad hurried past on his way to the dinosaurs, he was still wearing his cowboy hat. As soon as he was out of sight, Mum grabbed Robert's hand.

'This way, Lysander!'

Then they were running again – through Nursery Rhyme Land, past the Leaning Tower of Chimney Pots.

'Mum,' Robert puffed, 'The dinosaurs are the other way!'

A GAME OF PIRATES

'But we're pirates!' Mum called back, 'We're playing pirate hide-and-seek!'

Robert tried to slow her down.

'Mum, shouldn't we go and find Dad now? Mum, he'll be worried … Mum, he's going to be really cross.'

'Course he won't. We're on holiday,' Mum said brightly. 'Straighten your eye patch, we're playing pirates.'

'I want to be a cowboy,' he pulled on her hand. 'Mum, you told Dad we'd be by the styracosaurus.'

'Cowboys always leave a false trail.'

'But we're being pirates.'

'Then come on, me hearty. We've treasure to find.'

Robert held onto Mum's hand, and ran with her, too breathless for more questions. But his tummy was doing flips when he thought about Dad. Robert hated it when Dad got cross, especially when he got cross with Mum. He realised they were heading for the Main Gate, and his tummy flipped higher and faster.

The taxi was hot and smelt of stale feet and old plastic. Robert worried that his seat belt didn't fit properly, though Mum said it didn't matter. He felt sick and the window wouldn't open, but Mum was rummaging in her rucksack and Robert didn't want to bother her. Instead he sat very still and counted the strands of hair stretched across the driver's bald head and tried to get back his happy feeling.

He loved being on holiday with Mum and Dad, even though he and Mum were sleeping in one room and Dad was in another room with Claire. Robert was so happy just to be with Mum. But last night, after she tucked him in, Robert heard them shouting in Dad's room. He called out, but Claire came instead. Robert liked Claire and he liked living in the big house with her and Dad, but he wanted Mum. So he pretended to go to sleep until Claire went away. When Mum came at last she was crying, so Robert kept quiet. In the morning everyone pretended nothing had happened. They talked about Fantasy Chine instead. Claire said she was going shopping and Robert was glad because Mum was better when Claire wasn't around.

The shouting – that was why they were in the taxi. Mum stopped rummaging in the rucksack, pulled off her pirate gear and tucked her blonde hair under a red cap so Robert asked, 'Have we stopped being pirates now?'

Mum smiled that smile that made him feel loved and sick with worry all in one heartbeat. She leaned over and whispered, 'We're still pirates, but now we're shape-shifters too.'

Robert shivered at the thought.

Mum gently took off his eye-patch and headscarf, 'I love you, Lysander.' She kissed his nose. 'Now slip these on.'

A GAME OF PIRATES

By the time the ferry was ready for boarding, Robert and Mum were dressed in matching blue cagoules, and light brown shorts. Mum wore the red cap, Robert a denim beanie. His tummy had stopped doing flips and settled to a heavy feeling, like he'd swallowed a big stone.

Mum kept saying it was like *Pirates of the Caribbean*. Robert wanted to tell her the film had given him nightmares, but he just held onto her hand. Less than a week ago he'd boarded the ferry safe and warm in the back of Dad's 4x4, now he and Mum walked on open to a sky heavy with rainclouds, the metal gangway trembling under their feet. They huddled together on the top deck trying to keep out of the wind.

'I'm hungry. Mum, is it lunchtime?'

'Soon as we're underway, I'll get some sandwiches.'

Robert remembered something important. 'Dad's got your pills.'

Mum hugged him close. 'No he hasn't.'

'He's going to be so cross, Mum. And he's going to be really worried.'

'Then he shouldn't have tried to take you away from me.' Mum took off Robert's beanie and ran her fingers through his hair. 'Do you know where Los Angeles is?'

'It's on the western coast of the United States of America. It means City of Angels.' Robert said proudly. 'That's where Dad's new job is –' He paused. 'I'm not supposed to talk to you about it.'

'That's because Los Angeles is so far away I'd never see you again. I couldn't meet you from school on Friday nights. We couldn't have sleepovers. You'd forget all about me.'

'But Dad says you can come and stay with us. And we can come over for holidays.'

'Your Dad knows I'm not allowed in the States.' Mum knelt down on the deck in front of Robert and held his hands. 'Lysander, do you remember when you were little and I went to stay in that special hospital?'

Robert wriggled on his seat and shook his head. 'Not really.' Now she'd started talking, he wanted her to stop. 'Mum, please call me Robert.'

She carried on, 'I did some silly things and some bad things. I got into trouble with the police. I was very messed up and confused. That's why you had to go and live with Dad. Mums aren't allowed to mess up. If I was a dad it'd be like in the movies and everyone would say "Ahhh, but look how he loves his son ... give him another chance". But mums have to be perfect ... or they take your child away.' Mum rubbed her eyes with the back of her hand. 'If you go to Los Angeles, I won't be allowed to come and see you. And you won't be able to come and see me unless Dad brings you. And he won't.'

'He says he will.'

A GAME OF PIRATES

'He won't. Once Claire gets you both over there, she'll make sure of it.' Mum wrapped her arms too tightly around Robert's middle. 'You are the best thing, the one true, good thing in my life. You keep me sane. I won't give you up, Lysander.'

Robert thought, that's not my name. But he said, 'where are we going?'

Mum stood up and leaned on the rail, looking out to sea. 'Don't know,' she shrugged. 'We'll get a train somewhere. What an adventure!'

Robert didn't know the right thing to say, so he didn't say anything. They went to the buffet, but all the sandwiches had gone. Mum said he could have another ice-cream, but he didn't feel like ice-cream now. Back up on deck it started to drizzle. Robert shivered, counting the boats to take his mind off the cold, and wished Dad would come and give him a big, hairy bear-hug. Mum just sat staring ahead, so Robert held her hand tighter and tried to feel like a pirate. At last they reached the ferry terminal and the other passengers filed off. But Robert and Mum hung back, peering over the rail at the gangway below.

'Look,' Robert said. 'There's a policeman and a lady policeman coming on board.'

Robert and Mum ran to the other side of the ferry and squeezed down between the seats. She put her hand over his mouth and he felt it shaking.

A GAME OF PIRATES

Robert whispered, 'I think they can see us, Mum.' He could hear footsteps coming slowly across the deck, one step to every several of his heartbeats.

Mum stood up. Her cap had fallen off and her hair was messy around her shoulders. Robert stood up too. The lady policeman was just three rows of seats away. She looked a bit like Claire, taller than Mum with tidy brown hair in a sort of plaity bun. 'Over here, Gary!' she called over her shoulder. 'Lucy Baker?'

The policeman came running round the corner. He was older and a bit fat, but his voice was kind. 'Come on now, madam. Let's not upset the boy.'

Mum kissed Robert on his lips. Then she sprang, like a pirate princess, up onto the ship's rail, arms outstretched, waving an invisible cutlass.

Robert bit his lip to keep the tears in.

'Seems I must walk the plank,' she laughed. 'Farewell, Lysander my Love.'

Robert heard himself scream, 'Stop calling me that – MY NAME'S ROBERT!'

Mum stopped, balanced gracefully on one leg. She smiled her brightest smile. Robert saw her start to climb down.

He knew she was trying to climb down.

Whatever they said later, he always insisted Mum was climbing down.

She was climbing back down to him.

Room 516

Amy swore at the traffic on the M3 as the outside lane slowed to a limp. Away in the distance flashing blue and orange lights shone through the rain that had been threatening all day. She popped another couple of jelly babies into her mouth. Her teeth felt fuzzy – there'd been no time to brush them. And she was still wearing the uniform she'd been in since six that morning. Thank God the desk sergeant had noticed her shoes before she left the station. Vomit-splashed flatties – what a turn-on that would have been.

A truck rumbled past on her left, shaking the little yellow car and blurring the windscreen with

ROOM 516

spray. Driving rain, stop-start traffic, bruising juggernauts and boy-racers cutting her up – definitely not the way Amy had envisioned the evening would begin. But then, as she checked her rear view mirror, she glimpsed the glossy *Rose and Lily* carrier bag on the back seat. Amy smiled, eased into the middle lane, and pushed a Katie Melua CD into the player. By the time she wove through onto the M25, the nightmare of her ghastly day was sinking under dreams of the glorious night to come.

Almost an hour later Amy drove into the car park at the Heathrow Balmoral Hotel and squeezed her middle-aged hatchback between a spotless 4x4 and an equally shiny cabriolet. She checked her phone for texts, Greg was already there: 'Room 516. Come straight up.' Designer carrier in one hand and overnight bag on her other shoulder, Amy sprinted through the rain past the rows of cars, her focus on the shiny glass entrance to the five star hotel, eyes blinkered against the ugliness of the surrounding airport buildings, ears closed to the rumbling of car engines and the roaring of jets.

The hotel lobby resembled a plushly furnished jungle. As Amy strode towards the elevator, a pride of business men glanced over their laptops and newspapers, while, at the sight of her police uniform, two suspiciously glamorous flamingos fluttered into the Ladies' and a dark haired predator in a sharp suit slid into the shadows of the bar. Amy's professional brain filed the scene away behind thoughts of Greg.

Alone in the elevator, she closed her eyes, picturing herself in Greg's arms, his fingers gently unpinning her long dark hair. She imagined the evening ahead. Sipping champagne in the bath, her body tantalisingly hidden beneath fragrant bubbles. His gasps of admiration as she appeared, hair and makeup immaculate, draped in her beautiful new dress – the most expensive piece of clothing she'd ever owned. The envious glances as Greg escorted her into dinner in the Balmoral's internationally acclaimed, Michelin-starred restaurant. The anticipation as they enjoyed a nightcap in the hotel bar. And the delicious agony of that long journey back up to their room. Amy shivered with excitement.

Stepping from the elevator, she followed the corridor to room 516. The hotel was arranged around an atrium: the expensive rooms facing outwards with views of the planes, the really expensive ones looking inwards onto a paradise of restaurants, swimming pools and leafy lounges. Room 516 faced inwards. Heart thumping, face flushed, knickers just a little damp, Amy composed herself – and knocked.

Greg held the door open and reached for her hand, guiding her into the room. 'Where've you been? I thought you'd stood me up.'

His smile had its usual effect on Amy's composure. 'I couldn't get away,' she stammered.

ROOM 516

'The traffic was awful. I didn't have time to get changed. Or shower. Or anything.'

Still smiling, Greg handed her a glass of champagne. 'You look amazing – arresting! What was it today? Drugs cartel? International crime syndicate?'

Amy took a quick sip, her overnight bag still on her shoulder, the *Rose and Lily* carrier clasped in her hand. 'Nothing like that.' Another sip. 'Actually, it was really sad. There was this woman ... she'd snatched her own son. It was awful, she –'

'Poor you.' Greg held out his arms. 'Come here.'

Amy hesitated. 'I really need a shower. I want to get changed before dinner.'

'Uh uh. I've been waiting long enough. Five ... six years?'

'Eight.'

'Eight years? You can't ask me to wait another minute. Christ, Amy, you're every man's fantasy. Beautiful face, fantastic body. And that uniform ... Hang on a minute –' Greg fumbled in his jacket pocket, pulled out his phone, and looked at the number. 'I need to get this – it's the boss man.' He walked over to the desk. 'Max, yep. I'm all ears.'

Amy put her bags by the wardrobe and sat on the enormous bed. She bounced a little. It was bigger than a king-size. Was it an Emperor? Master-of-the-Universe? The pillows and cover were dented where Greg had been lying, an almost empty bottle of Moet on the bedside table. She looked around the room: deep-pile carpet, oversized pictures of exotic flowers on the walls and the bedspread. And that big picture window she'd seen on the hotel website. It was all like something off the TV, but better. I love it, she thought. She looked over at Greg.

'And I love you,' she whispered under her breath.

Greg was busy talking on the phone and tapping at his laptop. Amy gazed at him unnoticed, remembering back to the spring morning she'd arrived at the scene of her first office break-in, and fallen for the sales manager's charm and good looks. Six foot two of alpha male with the features of a cheeky schoolboy. And a smile to thaw even the coolest and most earnest of WPCs. When he asked her out Amy eagerly agreed, even though she knew it was unprofessional. Then on their first and only date, they bumped into Louise.

Greg was staring at his laptop. He loosened his tie, fastened and unfastened his watch. 'Dinner? Sorry, Max, I've got a shed load of preparation to do for tomorrow. Nah, I'll probably just work through.' He looked across at Amy and winked. 'I could be at it all night.' Amy blushed. 'Yep… yep… OK, boss. See you in the morning.'

Greg hung up the call and closed his lap-top. Then he grinned and rubbed his hands, 'Right, where were we?'

'I really need a shower.' Amy protested, moving towards the bathroom.

He caught her arm and shook his head, 'I don't think so.'

ROOM 516

'And dinner – I haven't eaten since lunchtime. Just jelly babies.'

'I'll order room service. Later.'

'But...'

'I want you just like this. Come here, you sexy lady. Read me my rights...' The phone rang again and Greg glanced at the number. 'Shit!'

He walked away across the room.

'Hello, darling. You got my message? Yeah, mix up with the flights. Oh, you know … one of those dreary airport hotels – could be anywhere.' Greg fiddled with his watch. 'There's no point, Louise, I'm on the seven am. I'd get home and have to drive straight back again.' He lowered his voice a little. 'Me too. Of course I do.' He gave a gentle, intimate laugh. 'Is that Olly? Put him on. Wotcha mate, why aren't you in bed?'

Amy watched the lies dribble from Greg's mouth as he chatted with his five-year-old son. She pictured golden haired Louise in her new conservatory kitchen, photogenic baby in her arms, all her energy divided between the children, too distracted to notice her husband's attention wandering as she droned on about the school run and potty training. Louise might not notice but some other woman would. Some other woman had, and been quick to take advantage. She walked over to the window and rested her forehead on the cool glass, forcing her thoughts onto the tropical paradise below, onto the Heathrow Balmoral's elegantly plumaged customers and a world

ROOM 516

untouched by sordid everyday problems. Her gaze lingered over the Caribbean blue of the swimming pool. Oh, to dive into that pool and wash everything clean again.

'OK, sweetheart, I'll call you from Hamburg tomorrow. Sweet dreams, my darling.'

Greg hung up and Amy felt suddenly cold inside, her hands slightly shaking. She closed her eyes for a moment. Then she snapped them open and WPC Amy Clarke spun around. 'Greg Dixon? Hold it right there. I need you to help with my enquiries.'

Greg's open mouth twisted into a smirk. 'Oh yes, officer? How can I be of assistance?'

'This is a stop and search.' She looked at him steadily, unsmiling. 'Remove your clothes.'

Minutes later, Greg lay naked, stretched out on the enormous hotel bed, handcuffed to a wall light just above his head.

'It's a very serious matter, sir,' Amy said sternly, one foot on the bed as she untied her shoe lace. 'You've been found in possession of an unauthorised erection.'

Greg groaned and struggled theatrically. Amy removed her tie and unbuttoned her shirt. 'Unattended erections are prohibited under the 2005 penile code.' She let her shirt fall from her shoulders and started on her trousers. 'It will have to be attended to.'

ROOM 516

Greg writhed and closed his eyes, then opened them again quickly in case he was missing anything. Amy stood before him in supermarket underwear.

'Oh Jesus Christ,' he gasped. 'Constable Amy, you are amazing. I married the wrong fucking sister.'

Amy stepped out of the shower and wrapped herself in sumptuous executive towelling. She brushed her teeth, dropping the toothbrush in the bin on top of her discarded underwear. Her hands had stopped shaking, and she dried herself, rubbing roughly at her skin until it smarted, then smoothed on a layer of expensive moisturiser, courtesy of the Heathrow Balmoral. The flesh was firm under her palms, toned and disciplined – a body in its prime. Her face was OK too, quite pretty when she smiled. But Amy knew her smile was only a second rate imitation of Louise's. She was just an oversized, badly drawn Louise in a dark wig – the nose too big, the eyes too small, and with far less to smile about.

Louise was only fifteen months younger, but somehow fifteen times smarter, prettier, more popular. Amy didn't want to think about her younger sister, but Louise butted in anyway, as she always did. As she had from the moment she was born, when the best part of everything that had been Amy's – toys, books, even her parents – was passed on to Louise.

At school Louise was better at everything except sport. 'I'm more interested in sportsmen,' she'd smile. Amy quickly adapted to life as Louise's sister – to not competing, to not coveting what Louise had, and to not aspiring to anything that Louise might want. Until Greg.

'I found him,' she muttered. 'You stole him from me.'

Badly drawn Louise whispered inside her head, 'He's not such a prize. You're better off without.'

Amy slowly dried her hair, and hid the betrayals of the day under a layer of makeup. Then she put on her best undies, took a deep breath and opened the door.

Greg was still on the bed, but his erection had long gone. A great white hunter caught in his own trap. 'You stupid cow!' he bellowed, rattling the handcuffs. 'Get these off me!'

Amy made a professional assessment: mid forties, carrying a bit too much weight around the middle, pretty-boy face showing signs of sagging and wrinkles.

'Calm down, sir,' she said, picking up her uniform and folding each item carefully. 'We don't want a scene, do we? Especially not a scene where someone bursts in and finds a middle-aged man compromised in a hotel room with all his flab on show.'

Greg quietened down, but he was far from calm. 'What the fuck are you playing at?' he snarled. 'I've spent a fortune on this room.'

ROOM 516

Amy put the uniform in her overnight bag. 'Come off it, Greg. You've got an account code for this sort of thing.' She pulled a red silk dress out of the *Rose and Lily* carrier and held it up for him to admire. 'I bought this for our romantic dinner.'

'What were you expecting? Hearts and flowers?' Greg sneered. 'I was doing you a favour. You've been sniffing round me for years.'

'And you thought you'd bag the complete set of Clarke girls.'

Amy bit the tag off her new dress with strong, white teeth. She pulled the cool silk over her head, letting it fall and smoothing the fabric into place over her belly and hips.

'This would be wasted on room service. I'm in the mood for something expensive – I'll charge it to room 516.'

She gathered up her belongings, then paused to pick up Greg's phone.

'Oh and don't worry, I'll make sure someone rescues you in time for your flight. Now who will it be – the boss man or Louise?'

The Man in the Shadows

I am the one who watches from the shadows. Tantalised by the aroma of your darkest secrets. Secrets you will never tell your lover. God forbid you'd tell your parents. Pray that your children never find them out. Perhaps you daren't even tell yourself. But, if I ask it, you will tell me.

Don't turn around – I know you know I'm here. You don't know who I am, or what I am, but you know I'm here. Keep walking if you can, maybe I'll let you go. Perhaps I'll sniff a juicier morsel and leave you for another day ... Perhaps.

Or maybe I will draw you to me as I am drawn to you. You might take a short cut through the shadows. Step into the dark of a waiting taxi. Or stop for a drink in this dimly lit bar.

Here, in the shadows of the bar, time slows to a series of spot-lit tableaus. Groups of business men bragging over their beer, proud of their petty vices. A couple of working girls looking for customers. Vulgar sins reeking of chain-store scent. Nothing to get my teeth into.

Until she arrives. Framed in the entrance. Backlit by the bright world beyond, like a dark angel. That dress – red silk, the colour of lust. Her hair is bitter chocolate, luscious as a Hollywood vampire. Promising, most promising. Across the bar, the men mutter their lascivious intentions and the whores curse the competition.

Eyes closed, I breathe her in. Blood and betrayal, a delightfully piquant blend. I open my eyes. I smile. She hesitates, confused, sees me alone at this table: young and handsome, affluent, well dressed. Virile and commanding. She smiles at me. My eyes guide her here, into the shadows. A small gesture of my hand and she sits. A barely perceptible tightening of my mouth and, unaware, she inclines her body towards mine.

The waiter brings cognac. She sips, and speaks her sins through tainted lips. Jealousy, sex, familial rivalry. Meagre fare meagrely spiced, though her tears are abundant. Boredom beckons; I yawn and my spell begins to break. Then she looks into my eyes and I see something unexpected. She whispers and I hear a half-forgotten phrase.

'I'm so ashamed. I would do anything to put it right.'

Not self-indulgent guilt, not fear of consequences, but genuine contrition. A need to make amends. As I am gripped by a barely remembered excitement, she starts to turn away. No! I must not let this one go.

I touch her flushed cheek with the cold tip of my outstretched finger. Her eyes grow black. She is mine again. I breathe. Take my hand, my beauty, come with me. Miles from this shadowy bar. Years before you were born. Close your eyes, I will tell you a tale.

A summer afternoon. On a cliff above a bay a young man, not much older than a boy, sat on a stile, cradling his guitar and singing a song of perfect love. Love that he, for all his tender years, already knew was too perfect to last. The song reached into a dark place within his heart and he savoured the sadness.

The young man was on the fringes of a technicolour of youth. Brilliant hues stretching away to the horizon, up onto the hills, down into the sea. One hundred and fifty thousand beautiful people. Singing and swaying, dancing and digging each other, smoking weed and feeling the love.

At his feet sat a multicoloured congregation. Summoned by his song of perfect love, thirty eager faces gazed up at the singer. The jeans that covered his long legs were faded, frayed and worn, but clean.

THE MAN IN THE SHADOWS

The t-shirt that covered his lean chest shone a vivid orange sun tie-dyed into a twilit sky. His hair was a dark curtain that hid the golden ring in his ear and the silver cross at his throat. The girls on the ground watched his fingers caressing the guitar and each felt she must love him or her heart would break. So many hearts he knew would be broken or tattered before they were full grown.

The crowd before the young man spread, sat in rapt silence. He hid his tears in the shadows of his hair, in emotional solitude veiled by his music. Until he sang the last word, strummed the last note, lifted his dark brown eyes and smiled with secret irony.

A pale, ginger-haired girl in a crocheted poncho clapped her hands above her floppy-brimmed hat. 'Fab-u-lous!'

'Beautiful vibes, man!' A pair of matching afros, like conjoined twins beneath an oversized trench-coat, lifted their fingers in peace salutes.

'Really dig your music.' Two boys in loon pants and maroon waistcoats waved their hash pipes and drifted away.

The young man smiled his smile as, one by one, his audience departed. He waited until he was alone then jumped down from the stile, resting his guitar against the hedge.

'How sad you are, Davey.'

He hadn't noticed the girl who spoke. She stared past him, out to sea, so slight she came barely to his shoulder. He looked down at her. She wore a purple scarf around her head over long flaxen hair tied in schoolgirl braids. A single strand of coloured love-beads hung over a thin peasant blouse, white as infant teeth, that cradled her scarcely formed breasts. Her shorts were made from an old pair of jeans, cut so high he could see the soft curves at the top of her thighs. Her feet were bare. She looked too young to be there alone. 'My name is Maud,' she said, looking up at him. And her eyes gleamed with the embers of something ancient.

Davey took the girl's outstretched hand and they walked away from the festival crowds, over the cliff top and down into a long bay. Maud sat on the sand and he sat beside her, his arm around her slender shoulders.

'Tell me your sins, Davey,' she said.

And Davey told her. He told her about Sandy, the girl he'd met in the coffee bar one rainy Thursday. Sandy who still wore school uniform, but said she didn't have to wear her beret now she was in the sixth form. When he could afford it, they went to the movies; when he was short of cash, they sat in the park and Davey played his guitar and sang the love songs she'd inspired. His university friends teased him about dating a schoolgirl, but Davey didn't care. What if she didn't want to philosophise with his flatmates, or march against the war in Vietnam? He'd never been a part of that scene. Sandy made him feel clever and worldly. She was his muse and he was her mentor, shaping her for the adult world. He introduced her to all sorts of firsts: her first taste of brandy, her first joint, her first lay. She said Davey was her first love. Davey said he loved her too.

When Sandy told him she'd missed her period he felt oddly calm, calmer still when she missed the next. They agreed not to tell her folks, Davey had never been introduced, but they sounded like real squares, bound to kick up a fuss. A girl at the student union had the number of a clinic and the name of a doctor who'd help. Davey held Sandy's hand on the bus and in the waiting room. Afterwards, he tried to take her home, but she pushed him away and ran off crying. It was later that evening, as he sat in the student bar, tuning his guitar and downing his seventh pint of cider, that someone told him about the policeman who'd knocked at his digs.

Davey looked at Maud and drew in a deep breath. 'She was only fourteen. Thirteen when we met. I screwed one child then I made her abort another.'

'You did a very bad thing, Davey.'

'I'd do anything … anything … if there was anything I could do to put it right. I split before the police could find me. I haven't been back to my digs, or home to my folks. I'm really sorry for what I did, Maud, but I'm too ashamed to face them.'

The girl's mouth curved into a slow, sad smile. 'Do you really want to make amends? If you are truly penitent, I can help you.'

THE MAN IN THE SHADOWS

The sky was darkening with clouds. Davey thought of his backpack lying somewhere in a field, his guitar left leaning on a hedge beside a stile. They seemed so abstract. Maud shivered and Davey wrapped his arms around her, tried to surround her slight form and thin clothes with the warmth of his body.

'You must be freezing.'

'I'm always cold.'

Up on the cliff top, two figures with backpacks looked down into the bay. Davey jumped up and felt in his pockets.

'Wait here.'

Maud was on her feet in a moment, her arms reaching out to him, panic in her voice. 'Come back!'

Already half way up the cliff, Davey called over his shoulder, 'I'll only be a minute!'

When he returned to the beach, Maud was tucked against a rock, curled in a foetal ball, her head on her knees.

'Maud?'

She looked up, face wet with tears, and held out her hands to him like a loveless child.

'Don't cry, Maud. I wasn't running out on you. I traded some weed for this.' Wrung with tenderness, he wrapped a Mexican blanket around her and lifted her gently to her feet. 'Help me collect some driftwood so we can light a fire.'

THE MAN IN THE SHADOWS

They sat by the fire in silence. Davey wondered if Maud expected him to make love to her. He was relieved that she didn't make a move; although he sensed the girl was older than he, she looked disturbingly young. Gradually, the warmth of the day drained from the sand until it was cold as old bones. The sun seeped over the horizon and the waves were washed with black. Only the flames cast light and heat, reflecting in the bright colours of Davey's T-shirt and Maud's blanket, flickering into the shadows all around. Along the curve of the bay a handful of small fires lit the way back to the festival fields.

Davey pulled a little pouch from his jeans pocket. His long fingers rolled a joint, lit it and held it up to Maud's lips as she took a light drag. He sucked on it in turn, inhaling as deeply as he could, feeling his limbs grow languid, his mind release the last scrap of self determination. The fire glowed with unworldly brilliance as Davey surrendered his senses to the marijuana, stretching out his long legs, his head cradled in his arms. Maud lay beside him, resting against his chest, the blanket pulled up around her ears and down over her bare toes.

'Do you truly wish penitence, Davey?' The question was so quiet and clear, it seemed her voice was inside his head.

'Can you help me?' Davey whispered back.

He felt the tension in her slight child's body as she replied, 'I believe we can help each other. Close your eyes. I will tell you a tale.'

THE MAN IN THE SHADOWS

Maud's story played in Davey's consciousness like images on celluloid. A patched blue dress and white apron, long plaits tucked under a mop cap. A pair of bright young eyes, alight with love, gazing from a leaded window. Below in a courtyard, a handsome footman stealing a kiss from a lady's maid, pressing a note into her palm. The eyes at the window glittering green with jealousy. A money bag hidden under a servant's paliasse. An innocent disgraced, taken by the constable, despatched to the colonies.

Wandering by moonlight, the girl in white and blue. Across fields, along lanes. Night after lonely night, begging the moon for forgiveness. Until at last in the shadows of a wood, a man with ancient eyes and a tale to tell. A man promising a chance to make amends – a task for the truly penitent. Shadows enveloping them. And the girl emerging alone, her eyes red with a strange and hungry fire.

Then a giddying spiral of people, cities, countries. Faces twisted with greed, with lust, with hate. And the girl, like a pied piper for the damned, drawing them to her, feeding their sins to the furnace in her eyes. French cuisine served up by Madame La Guillotine. Salty rancid meat on slave ships bound for the colonies. Charred and bitter fruit in the smoking remains of tribal villages. Now following armies across Europe, nibbling on the casual crimes of war. Now banqueting with the commandant of an Eastern concentration camp. Tasting tapas with a grey old man in a dark Brazilian bar. Within her slender frame her soul is stenched with sin. And still she hungers.

What becomes of the sinners? Her touch is a lance, drawing their evil out. What then is left? For some, absolution, a clean wound and a chance to heal. For the others? In a dark Victorian lodging house, a cloaked man opens his black bag and lays out his medical instruments. By morning he is drained of so much evil all that remains is the myth.

Night time faded into dawn as the sea became blue again and the sand warmed to a golden brown. Davey shuddered back to a consciousness wracked by the nauseous aching hangover of a bad trip. The Mexican blanket was pulled up so high all he could see was the purple of Maud's scarf and a lock of her hair. He opened his mouth to rouse the sleeping girl, but no words would come.

One by one, the visions returned to him, not the foggy remembrances of a dream, but sharp and eloquent, ringing with all their original cruelty and horror. Twisted ebony limbs, shiny with sweat and blood. Lips that still screamed after their body was sliced away. The smell of burning babies. Davey reached out to Maud, seeking to comfort and be comforted, to feel the security of another human form. The blanket sank beneath his arm.

He called her name, looked all around, up and down the beach. He stood up, awkwardly, limbs stiff

THE MAN IN THE SHADOWS

from his bed on the sand, and the blanket fell away. Beneath it a scrap of purple wrapped around a braid of faded hair, and a string of beads upon a pile of ashes, the colour of bones.

Davey's knees buckled. As he sank down onto the sand, the silver cross fell from his throat into the glowing embers of the driftwood fire.

And so I sit here, the man in the shadows. Sniffing out sins in this dimly lit bar with a beautiful girl dressed in red silk seated beside me. My palate is cosmopolitan. I've tasted flesh barbequed with napalm. Feasted on titbits of Chinese fare with a side order of fear from the Cultural Revolution. Licked the cream from the profits of human trafficking across Europe. And filled up on fast-food loathing in every state of the USA.

Now I look into the eyes of the girl in the red dress. Her face is pale, her eyes focussed far away from this bar, somewhere by the sea, in a dream of my making. Weariness weights my limbs, shudders down my back bending my spine. The cure is drastic, but I am almost free.

I whisper inside her head, 'If you are truly penitent, then I can help you make amends. We can help each other.'

Maud's love-beads are tucked inside my breast pocket. I think of her and forgotten tears kiss my cheek. I picture the girl beside me one hundred years from now – her beauty preserved, her soul stretched beyond endurance. I imagine her driven by this hunger, wandering the world, seeking out the darkest corners of the human heart.

I close my eyes and she murmurs her way back to reality. Back to the safety of the bar. Eyes open, I drink my brandy with one swallow, kiss her hand, and walk away.

I am the one who watches you from the shadows. Perhaps, after all, your sins are not so great. A snack, that's all. Leaving you weary, but at peace – and me far from satisfied. Or maybe I'm bloated now, I needn't feast again for days, sin was your whole existence and you are gone.

Or perhaps you are truly penitent, looking for a way to make amends. Perhaps we can help each other.

The View from the Penthouse Apartment

She leaned over the railing and looked down at the world dizzyingly far below. The marina, the river, cars hurrying home over the bridge – all a hundred feet or more far, far below. Lights shifted and whirled before her eyes, distorted by the prism of the rain: lamps blinking on masts, bright windows of offices in the City beyond, headlights flickering through the dusk. Dusk, the perfect time to enjoy the roof garden. Perfect but for the rain that had been falling all day, and her life that had been free falling for months. She held onto the railing, slippery with rain water, and climbed up onto the parapet for a better look at the view.

THE VIEW FROM THE PENTHOUSE APARTMENT

Amanda had woken in the late afternoon. It must have been the rain, clattering like nails against the sliding glass doors. Thank God the thick velvet curtains were keeping the worst of the day at bay. Her head throbbed on the pillow; not even swansdown could cushion this hangover. She stretched out a cramped arm for a glass of water, but the lacquered antique cabinet, one of a very expensive pair sourced by a very exclusive antiques dealer, offered only dust and a clump of crumpled tissues. Amanda scrabbled one up to wipe her gummy lips.

She rolled into the centre of the emperor-sized bed, legs tangled in Egyptian linen that felt wrinkled and crusty. Amanda didn't know when it had last been washed; she hadn't washed herself for three days. The only reason to get out of bed was this grating thirst. She pushed away the covers and inched her body to the side of the bed, manoeuvring one leg at a time over the edge, and easing her bones along.

'Lights,' Amanda croaked and the recessed spots above her head lit up dimly, 'more... more... more... more...' she mumbled, then, 'Oh shit – less. Less!'

The marble floor of the wet room was cool on her bare feet. Amanda let the tap run, then filled her cupped hands and drank. The cold water burned her throat, and she spluttered and coughed herself upright in front of the mirror. At first she thought she was looking at her mother: those expressionless eyes and disappointed mouth. No, Amanda

THE VIEW FROM THE PENTHOUSE APARTMENT

concluded with a body blow of self-pity, her mother had never looked this rough. She stared at her once sleek auburn crop ruined by greasy grey roots and frizzy neglected ends, peered into the baggy red eyes, searching for herself behind that mask of sagging flesh, then broke eye contact and focussed over her right shoulder. To the luxurious massaging jets of the power-shower.

Amanda pushed and turned all the buttons and dials, but no cleansing water flowed. She sank to the floor beside a fuzz of matted hair and pulled at a towel to dry her face. The towel was damp and smelled of unwashed bodies so she used her nightdress instead, realising with a shudder that she was wearing one of Owen's t-shirts.

'It's just for a while, Amanda. I need some time alone.'
'But I'm away working all week. I'm hardly ever here.'
'You know, when a man hits his mid-forties...'
'I've made it into my fifties without a midlife crisis, Owen.'
'I just need to experience other things. I married too young.'
'Too young? But – '
'I just need to see what else the world has to offer.'

Amanda tore the t-shirt over her head and used it to wipe up the dust and hair, her joints wincing against the cold, hard tiles. Being careful not to look in the mirror, she reached for the zebra-striped silk robe that hung beside the door and shuffled back through the bedroom and into the lounge.

THE VIEW FROM THE PENTHOUSE APARTMENT

The lounge, a large, double-height space with an entire wall of glass opening onto the roof garden, was as still as a museum, the only signs of life an empty whisky bottle and stained crystal tumbler. Black burnt-velvet cushions were arranged with showroom perfection on oversized sofas, upholstered in a shade marketed as Ethiopian ecru. An eighteen inch facsimile of Pompon's polar bear, a parting gift for her years as Chief Executive of the Paris office, was positioned precisely in the centre of the black onyx coffee table; glossy books and magazines stacked in geometrically neat piles on the shelf below.

But the onyx was dulled by a layer of dust, the desert parchment carpet flecked with unidentifiable specks of fluff. And the magnificent wall of glass was smeared and stained, blighting the view that Amanda had fallen for when she first viewed the penthouse with Owen on her arm.

'TV on.' Amanda perched on the sofa as a section of the wall opposite morphed into the 24 hour news channel, revealing a thirty-something brunette who was chatting brightly about the state of the stock market. Amanda sighed and ran her fingers along the smooth back of the polar bear. She closed her eyes.

'I'd like to add my personal thanks, Amanda, for the wonderful job you've done here at the Paris office. The latest in a long line of successes, I believe: New York, Copenhagen, Sydney. I expect you're looking forward to winding down a bit.'

THE VIEW FROM THE PENTHOUSE APARTMENT

'I'm not retiring, Marcus.'
'Of course not.'
'I wanted to stay on.'
'Yes, yes. But if we're going to continue to grow the European business in today's technology climate we need an injection of youthful thinking. Sebastian's only thirty-two, but we think he's really going places.'
'And I'm going nowhere?'
'Very droll, Amanda. You're going to Middlesbrough.'

When Amanda opened her eyes, the thirty-something brunette had been replaced by a twenty-something blonde in a tight navy dress who predicted plenty of autumn sunshine across the Home Counties with maybe a light shower in places. Amanda looked at the rain stoning the penthouse windows.

She wandered across to the kitchen. Her bare toes, clammy from her three day refuge in unconsciousness, slicked up crumbs from the riven slate floor. The neglect was more obvious in here: unmopped spills, sticky rings from cups and glasses, rancid odours around the bin. Amanda pulled the last clean tumbler from the cupboard and filled it at the sink. This time she sipped the water, letting it gently soothe her throat. There was a cramping in her stomach; she should eat something, food might make her feel better. Food and coffee. Amanda opened the fridge – well, maybe just coffee. She picked up a carton of milk, sniffed it and pulled a face – black coffee.

'For heaven's sake, Amanda. How can a woman of your age be so useless around the home? Thank goodness for Owen. The man's a saint to put up with you.'

'Perhaps it has something to do with my executive salary and bonus package, Mum.'

'Well, it's not for your youth and beauty is it? A handsome man like that married to an older woman – you'd better keep your wits about you.'

Granite surfaces magnified the hissing of the kettle; the brightly lit water inside was like bubbling acid to Amanda's vulnerable eyes. She left Owen's cafetiere in the cupboard, tipping a teaspoon of instant coffee into an Art Deco mug and adding another spoonful plus two sugars for an extra kick. Her hand shook as she carried it back to the sofa, pausing to scrub the underside of her feet against the carpet.

The rain was still pelting against the windows, but the women on the news channel were as bright as they could be. The coffee certainly delivered the sought-after kick – Amanda sat with one hand on her head trying to keep her brain still and the other pressed against her heart to keep it from leaping out of her body, wondering if she could possibly die from an overdose of caffeine on an empty stomach. Breathing hard, she went in search of painkillers.

THE VIEW FROM THE PENTHOUSE APARTMENT

Owen's t-shirt lay on the wet room floor between Amanda and the medicine cabinet. She kicked it out of the way, found the remnants of a pack of paracetamol lodged behind her HRT pills and gulped them down with handfuls of water. Behind her own ghastly reflection, the power-shower mocked her. She smelt bad; she felt disgusting. She must get clean. She needed a plumber, but how did you find one? Owen always took care of these things, one of the advantages of marrying a man who was happy to stay and look after the home. Of course he had his own work; he'd made quite a success of his photography and that little camera shop. The shop she'd bankrolled for him. He still hadn't called. Perhaps he'd sent a text.

The spiral stairs to the mezzanine were an ordeal for Amanda's creaking knees, but she hauled herself up by the wrought iron banister and made it safely to the study she shared with Owen at the top. Her computer bag lay on the larger of the his-and-hers solid oak desks, where she'd abandoned it days before. Her mobile phone was stuffed in the side pocket, the battery completely flat. Amanda jostled everything out of the bag looking for the charger. Last time she'd used it was in the hotel in Middlesbrough.

'Amanda? It's late, you should be in bed.'
'Owen, I've been trying you all evening.'
'Oh? How's the frozen North? Natives friendly?'

THE VIEW FROM THE PENTHOUSE APARTMENT

'Mutinous. Half the office wanted the job themselves. They're already sticking the knife in. I want to come home.'

'Uh-uh. Not without a golden handshake, my darling. Thirty years service down the drain?'

'I can't do this anymore, Owen.'

'Get a good night's sleep, silly. You'll feel better in the morning. See you Friday.'

By Sunday night, Owen had gone. Amanda called the office in Middlesbrough and left a message that she had a viral infection, then she proceeded to self medicate with whisky, vodka and anything else with a significant alcohol content that she could find in the apartment.

The far wall of the mezzanine was devoted to a display of Owen's black and white photographs in discretely expensive frames. Amanda hurled her mobile at them. It ricocheted into a set of bookshelves packed with glossy volumes on photography, and boxes of old prints. She pulled these off the shelves, as many at a time as she could hold, and flung them over the balcony. She picked up an alabaster frame from Owen's desk and threw it as hard as she could at the TV below. She heard the screen crack, the missile rebound, and her Parisian polar bear skid and scrape across the black onyx. Amanda peered down at the mess and laughed. And cried.

She went downstairs to assess the damage. The picture frame was only slightly chipped, Owen and

THE VIEW FROM THE PENTHOUSE APARTMENT

Amanda still grinned from across the years in all their wedding day naivety.

'I'll call.'
'Are you moving in with Becky?'
'Becky?'
'She's got two young children. You said we didn't need children. You said you didn't want them, they'd ruin everything. You persuaded me...'
'Maybe I was too young to take them on before. I feel I've really grown up since I met Becky.'

Amanda felt a familiar stab in her ovary, the useless one the surgeon had left behind the year before. She picked up the polar bear and examined its ruined nose. Paris had been the pinnacle of her career; even at the time, she had known that whatever came afterwards would be the start of the long slide back down. Just as she knew the job in Middlesbrough would be hell: guerrilla warfare with a forty-plus subordinate who thought he deserved her job, his thirty-year-old deputy already plotting to clamber over both their professional carcasses.

As for Owen, in retrospect, Amanda was surprised he hadn't strayed before, maybe he had. But he might yet be back. The reality of life with a mummy who wasn't so yummy on a daily basis, combined with the demands of her small and implausibly adorable children, would certainly challenge Owen's aspirations. Or perhaps the financial pressures of a business already under attack from technology and talented amateurs would send him back into Amanda's arms. Provided, of course, she was still able to offer the penthouse lifestyle.

The lounge was a mess. Amanda made a pile of the books, stuffing stray pictures randomly back into boxes. Amongst Owen's professional shots she found a few old snaps of her own and carried a small black and white photo over to the window for a clearer look. The sky was still dark with rain, the image was blurry and Amanda couldn't find her glasses, but she could make out a big floppy-brimmed hat and a young girl's face beneath. Her memory added the colours: the hat green, the face pale and freckled, half-hidden behind round red sunglasses, her hair ginger, and the crocheted poncho that covered her shoulders all the colours of the rainbow.

August, 1969. The first holiday without her parents. She and a friend had taken backpacks and a small tent to the Isle of Wight. The first time she saw Dylan live. The first time she smoked a joint and danced naked on a beach in the rain. The drugs made her throw up and she caught a cold when the light summer shower turned torrential. Then Dylan was late and his set was a real anticlimax. But it didn't matter. None of it mattered. That little photograph held the sweetness of forgotten freedom. A time when the world was painted in cheap, bright colours instead of expensive, designer neutrals. When she

THE VIEW FROM THE PENTHOUSE APARTMENT

dreamed of seeing the world – not just the view from its five star hotels and expensive apartments.

'Travelling? Don't be ridiculous, Amanda. You are going straight back to school.'

'But, Mum, Zak said I could tag along wi– '

'Zak? That afro-headed creature who kept calling you Mandy? We didn't fork out on a private education for you to slum-it around round the world with some unwashed dropout. You'll end up on drugs ... or worse.'

'But, Mum –'

'Be quiet, you silly girl. You are going straight back to school and then you are going to get a proper job. You are not going to throw your life away.'

Amanda cried. For the girl in the floppy brimmed hat and her lost youth; for the woman in the zebra striped robe and her lost life. For the rain without rainbows, the fading of the sunshine and music. For other women's children and the children she had never conceived. For years passed and grey years ahead. Then she went out to the roof garden.

A hundred feet or more above the world below, Amanda pushed back her dripping hair with trembling hands and tilted her face up to the sky so that rain and tears became indistinguishable. Swaying a little, she looked back at the sculptural outline of the penthouse and its tall windows, at the sour,

119

THE VIEW FROM THE PENTHOUSE APARTMENT

wrinkled bed within. She peeled off her zebra-print robe and let it fall to the street below.

Amanda climbed down from the parapet and held up her arms, letting the water wash over her body.

Then, naked, she danced in the rain.

Gingerbread

It all began with the house. Inviting as a freshly baked treat in the September sunshine. Cranberry red roof tiles, walls the colour of rich fruitcake, fretworked gables like piped icing, and little potted bay trees trimmed into green lollipops standing guard beside the dark chocolate front door. Everything about it looked good enough to eat. Everything about it looked too good to be true. Including the handwritten sign that read:

*'Basement flat for rent.
Very reasonable terms for the right tenants.'*

'I know! It's almost too good to be true,' Gee Geoffrey laughed into her mobile as she hurried back down Holly Hill towards the High Street. 'Right on the edge of the Heath, down a little private road I didn't even know was there. Oh, Babe, I'd just about despaired of ever finding anything we could afford in Hampstead.' She adjusted her oversized sunglasses, flicking away a strand of honey-coloured hair. 'It's only a studio, I know, but it's big and really nice. Separate kitchen, and an ensuite with a bath and a shower ... Meet me in the Frognall Arms as soon as you can. I'll get some cash. We'll take a deposit round before someone else snaps it up.'

A stylish basement flat that was cosy yet light, tucked away in a prime corner of Hampstead, with parking beside the main house plus its own private access through a pretty walled garden – Gee clutched the prospect like a talisman, sipping her mineral water as the rest of the pub gradually became aware of the celebrity in their midst. She knew they saw what she wanted them to see: glamorous weathergirl engaged to handsome, upper-crust rugby pro; designer clothes and her picture in the gossip magazines. But she also knew that CityScape News was only interested in Gee Geoffrey's beautiful body and the brightness of her smile, not her beautiful mind and the brightness of her intellect. And that, despite her expensive attempts to emulate Fleur Taylor, the classy business correspondent, a recent lads' mag had placed Gee in the top three brainless blondes on Brit TV. As for the posh fiancée, Han's mother was openly scornful of Gee's unexceptional roots, and Han himself was currently sharing a flat with two teammates whose idea of a good night out involved a blitzkrieg of booze and babes that kept resulting in the wrong kind of publicity for Gee's media aspirations.

But she loved him, the big, handsome, laid-back hunk. Gee had all the ingredients for an amazing future for herself and Han – provided those ingredients didn't turn sour before she could get him away from his mates and his mother, and settled into the right postcode. The flat was not too good to be true, Gee decided, it was just the stroke of luck she had been waiting for.

'Hello again, Mrs Heksen. This is my fiancée.' Gee nudged Han up the red flag-stoned steps that led to the open front door. 'We've brought the deposit.'

A little white-haired woman with pink cheeks and eyes like currants behind horn-rimmed spectacles stood smiling in the doorway. She wiped her hands clean of flour on her red and white checked apron.

'Come in, my child,' her voice was soft with a Scandinavian lilt. 'Come into my kitchen.'

Mrs Heksen's kitchen was filled with the glow of the September sunset and the warm, spicy aroma of baking. She gestured for them to sit at the table and bustled to fill the kettle.

GINGERBREAD

'You will have a cup of tea with me? And a piece of gingerbread? Freshly baked.'

Han nodded enthusiastically.

Gee said, 'Thank you, Mrs Heksen. Han's always hungry.'

'Of course. A fine big man like your fiancée needs plenty of food.' She placed a blue and white china plate piled with gingerbread stars in front of him.

Han popped one into his mouth. Gee bit delicately into hers; the gingerbread was soft, sweet and fragrant; still warm from the oven.

'Oh, it's delicious,' Gee smiled.

'Mmm,' Han agreed with his mouth full. 'May I?' He popped in another.

'Why don't you show your young man around while I make the tea? You can use the kitchen stairs.' Mrs Heksen held aside a velvet curtain at the back of the kitchen revealing a twisting staircase leading down to the basement.

Han grabbed a handful of stars. Mrs Heksen's eyes twinkled as she selected three cups and saucers from a dresser laden with pretty china and cookery books. 'I hope you will like it here. I feel the house is delighted with you both.'

Two weeks later they moved in. Gee's chic, modern furniture blended beautifully with the older Scandinavian pieces provided by their landlady. After deploying Han to wrestle with a flat-packed bookshelf, Gee began sorting out the kitchen:

plugging in the microwave and filling the fridge and cupboards with ready meals and tins.

'Hello, child.' Mrs Heksen trod carefully down the steps from the garden balancing a freshly baked apple strudel on top of a casserole dish. 'For welcoming you both to your new home. Lam gryte – a lamb stew. And something sweet. You won't want to be cooking tonight.'

'Oh, how lovely. Thank you so much.'

Han appeared, a screwdriver in his hand. 'I thought I smelt something delicious. Mrs Heksen, will you marry me?'

The old lady wagged her finger at him. 'Now, now. You have a very pretty girl already.'

'But she can't cook.'

The first week brought lots of visitors.

On Monday night the rugby crowd accompanied Han back from the Frognall Arms.

'Ssh!' Gee warned as they galumphed through the garden and stumbled down the steps to the back door. 'Don't you dare wake our new landlady!' And she quietened them down with big slices of Mrs Heksen's chocolate cake.

On Wednesday Fleur Taylor, Gee's colleague and role model, dropped in. Fleur perched in a sculptural, latte-coloured leather chair sipping green tea and basking in the sunlight streaming through the high basement window.

'It's gorgeous, Gee. Small but perfect. Like a little fairytale cottage. And what a fabulous address.' She took another gingerbread star. 'Delicious! I didn't know you could cook.'

Han's mother timed her visit to coincide with her son's Friday training session.

'Oh. Is Han out?'

Gee sucked her teeth as her future mother-in-law checked for lapses of taste through her designer spectacles.

'That old woman could ask three times the rent she's getting from you.'

'Mrs Heksen doesn't need the money,' Gee explained. 'She likes us around for company, or if a light bulb needs changing or something.'

'Hm. It sounds too good to be true. Where's she from anyway? Did Han say she's Eastern European?'

'Norwegian. And a very kind old lady. We're lucky to have found her.'

Han's mother turned her attention to a carved pine nightstand. 'This house is much too big for an old woman on her own. Han says she keeps half of it locked up. Virtually lives in the kitchen. She'll put it on the market soon and then you'll both be out on your ears.'

Mrs Heksen's melting moments remained undisturbed in a tin in the kitchen.

GINGERBREAD

It was no surprise to Gee that her own family didn't visit.

'Dad doesn't really fancy the motorway,' her stepmother recited over the phone. 'And the train fares! Do you know how much it costs from Preston?'

As Gee hung up, she saw Mrs Heksen at the back door smiling over the top of a large blue and white flowered tin.

'I thought with all these visitors your cupboards might be running a little low.'

Pumpkin pie for Halloween, rich and tangy with a hint of orange and ginger. Chocolate brownies for Bonfire Night. Apple pie for Thanksgiving. And always a fruit tart or sponge pudding to have with their Sunday lunch, or a batch of cookies to top up the biscuit tin. As Christmas approached, the waistbands of Gee's skirts were under stress and the noticeable change to Han's physique prompted a stern warning from his coach to 'lay off the lard'.

'You are getting a bit tubby, Babe,' Gee said gently. 'Just cut out the cake for a bit.'

'I try to, but I can't help it. I think I'm addicted.'

Not wanting to offend Mrs Heksen, Gee smuggled tins of cakes and biscuits out of the basement flat and into the CityScape News studio.

'More treats!' Fleur Taylor called the crew over. 'Everyone, you simply must try Gee Geoffrey's angel kisses!'

Gee blushed as Fleur put an elegant arm around her shoulder.

'We're well and truly hooked, Gee. Promise you'll bake something special for the Christmas party next week.'

Gee was still pondering the problem that weekend as she carried the Saturday papers down the track at the side of the house, stepping her designer boots carefully around the icy puddles. She took an old key from her coat pocket and opened the heavy wooden door that led into the walled garden. Over by the vegetable patch Mrs Heksen, her checked apron tied over a long skirt and traditionally embroidered blouse, was cutting a sprig of something bright with red berries.

Gee cleared her throat. 'Mrs Heksen?'

No reply. Gee walked up the path, holding her coat around her. Mrs Heksen was singing softly to herself in another language.

'Mrs Heksen?' Gee touched her arm.

The old lady turned quickly, dropping her scissors and backing up against the high brick wall. Small yellow teeth showed between her parted lips and her eyes glittered like sharp coal.

'Oh, I'm so sorry. Did I startle you?' Gee picked up the scissors. 'You must be freezing out here.'

'I... I do not feel the cold.' Mrs Heksen waved her away.

GINGERBREAD

For the sake of the CityScape News Christmas party, and her own blossoming culinary reputation, Gee persevered. 'Were you cutting something for the kitchen? From this bush with the pretty berries?'

The old lady stepped away from the wall, the sprig in her left hand. 'This one? A Norwegian plant. You will not have heard of it'

'What's it called?'

Mrs Heksen frowned, 'Tysbast.'

'Tysbast?' Gee tried the name, adding with a laugh, 'No you're right, I've never heard of it. The berries look lovely. Bright like cranberries. Will you use them for cooking or decoration?'

'They are difficult to cook with. You must be very careful or they can be ... bitter.' Mrs Heksen thrust the sprig into her apron pocket and turned to another shrubby little plant. 'Ah, the lavender is finished for this year,' she sighed, 'but I have some dried flowers to make a lavender cake for tea – and a spare for the children who live downstairs.'

'We're hardly children.'

'Oh, but to me you are. Remember, I am very old. And I must make sure you eat well – since you are so "useless in the kitchen".'

Gee followed the old lady back to the house. 'About that ... Mrs Heksen, I need to ask you a huge favour. Would you teach me to cook?'

Mrs Heksen's cheeks flushed pink and her curranty eyes shone.

'Child, I have only been waiting for you to ask.'

GINGERBREAD

Gee examined the row of cookery books on the kitchen dresser.

'I really want to learn to cook proper meals for Han and me. Low-fat ones. We're both getting a bit tubby.'

The old lady considered Gee through her spectacles for a long moment, then she said, 'this modern trend to be all skin and bones is not good.'

Gee opened her mouth to remonstrate, but said instead, 'I don't know how you stay so slim, with all these wonderful sweet treats around you.'

'I keep busy always. I have what is called a high metabolism. This means I eat whatever I like and I never get fat.'

Mrs Heksen bustled to her store cupboard, and Gee realised it was true, she never did keep still for long. She also realised she had never seen the old lady take more than a nibble of food.

'Mrs Heksen, could we start with gingerbread? I'd really like to make some of those little stars for my office party. It's on Thursday.'

'Of course. This is very traditional. Very nice.'

'Which cookbook do we need?' Gee ran her finger along the spines. 'This is a funny little one – is it full of secret family recipes?' She held up a small, battered book with a dark red spine and loose pages crammed with handwritten notes. 'Oh, is this Norwegian?'

'These recipes are not for you.' Mrs Heksen plucked the book from Gee's hand and slipped it into her apron pocket. 'After all,' she added, 'you cannot read Norwegian, I think?'

Gee shook her head.

The old lady pointed to another book. 'That one, with the yellow cover. That has the little gingerbread stars. Your friends will be surprised you are such a good cook.'

If Mrs Heksen noticed Gee's blushes, she said nothing.

For the rest of the weekend, they baked and roasted and stewed until the windows were thick with steam and all the freezers and cake tins in the house were full.

'Child, you were born to cook,' the old lady insisted. 'I suspected this the moment you knocked upon my door. But how did you never discover it until now? Did you never cook with your mother?'

'I never knew my mother. My stepmother taught me to use the microwave.'

Mrs Heksen reached up and patted Gee's cheek. 'I never had a daughter to teach. I am happy and proud to be teaching you.'

The buffet at the CityScape News Christmas party was an outstanding success; Gee's gingerbread stars, Yule log bites and rich stollen slices providing a delicious testament to her skill as a baker.

'Have you considered,' Fleur Taylor suggested as she delicately licked chocolate cream from her perfectly manicured fingers, 'a cookery series? I know just the person who could help. Let's do lunch in the New Year.'

Even Han's mother grudgingly labelled Gee's Christmas cake 'quite pleasant', while the rugby crowd were so seduced by her piggy-figgy pudding they promised to send Han home early from the Frognall Arms for the next month if she'd make another.

Only Han was out of sorts.

'You're cooking all this fabulous stuff for other people,' he grumbled as they lay in bed on Christmas morning. 'All I get's lean grills and rabbit food.'

'Oh, Babe. You know what the coach said. If you get any fatter you'll be on the bench – if there's a bench strong enough to take you.' The amazing future Gee had been planning was at last within sight, and she wasn't about to let Han's expanding belly spoil the view. She sighed, 'I just don't understand why you're still piling on the pounds when I'm nearly back to normal. It's a mystery.'

The mystery was solved one foggy morning in the New Year. Gee had set off early to check out the new season collections in Knightsbridge, but was thwarted by a derailment on the Northern line. As she trudged back down the lane, Mrs Heksen's kitchen window glowed like a homing beacon through the gloom. Gee paused at the bottom of the red flagged steps, warmed by the sight of Mrs

GINGERBREAD

Heksen and Han at the kitchen table. One was nibbling on a piece of toast – the other was tucking into sausages, bacon, pancakes, syrup, fried tomatoes, fried eggs, fried potato and fried bread.

Gee stared. Han ate. Mrs Heksen slowly adjusted her horn-rimmed spectacles and looked out of the window straight at Gee. She held her gaze for a long moment.

Han hurried to open the door, blustering an apology. Gee barely heard what he had to say, she was watching Mrs Heksen and the old woman sat quietly, looking right back at her. The kitchen was warm with the smell of Han's breakfast. But Gee shivered.

'Please excuse us, Mrs Heksen,' she said as pleasantly as she could, leading Han the long way round, out of the front door, around the side of the house, through the garden, and down the steps, and through their own door into the basement apartment.

Gee looked down at Han's stockinged feet. 'I expect you usually sneak up the kitchen stairs when you want to stuff your face.' She slammed the door shut and locked it.

'It's not like that, Gee. Mrs Heksen asked me to fix a light upstairs. When I came down she'd cooked me breakfast.'

'You're on a diet. She knows you're on a diet.'

'Then why does she keep feeding me?'

GINGERBREAD

The problem, Gee decided, was how to curtail their landlady's misplaced generosity, while continuing to enjoy the benefits of the gingerbread house. Initially, she avoided any contact with Mrs Heksen, hoping not to have to make the first move. But her lunch date with Fleur Taylor's cookery contact was fast approaching and she needed the old lady back onside. So, after a couple of anxious days, Gee slunk up the twisting stairs to the kitchen and called from behind the velvet curtain.

'Hello Mrs Heksen? It's Gee.'

The kitchen was as warm and welcoming as ever, but Mrs Heksen wasn't there. Gee went into the hallway and called up to the floor above; then she tried the garden. Coming back into the house, she noticed a key in a door that was usually locked. Gee opened it and peered inside.

'Mrs Heksen?'

The room was quite dark, the tall window at the far end screened by heavy wooden shutters. As Gee's eyes adjusted she saw a formal dining room: a large table surrounded by chairs, a high sideboard, and an elaborately gothic chandelier. The furniture was all of a solid, dark wood, almost black, and ornately carved with strange, rather sinister, figures. Figures with grotesque faces, their limbs contorted around the frames of the chairs and the legs of the table. The floor was uncarpeted, the floorboards stained an unpleasantly dark red. She looked for a light switch, then realised there were no bulbs in the chandelier,

GINGERBREAD

only candles, stalactites of black wax that hung down to the tabletop. One chair, grander than the other twelve, stood at the head of the table. On the polished black surface before it lay a little book – the cookery book with the dark red spine that Gee had found on Mrs Heksen's dresser.

She held the book in the thin strand of light that squeezed through the window shutters and opened it carefully. It felt very old, the binding worn and fragile. The book was filled with handwritten notes that meant nothing to her, words such as: risted, polse, menneske. She recognised tysbast, the plant in the garden, and gryte – Mrs Heksen had brought them a lam gryte, lamb stew, on their first evening in the basement flat.

The room was cold with a strange smell that Gee didn't like, perhaps because Mrs Heksen kept it shut up. Mrs Heksen ... where was the old lady, anyway? She peeped through the gap in the shutters; Mrs Heksen was climbing the steps to the front door. Gee slipped out of the dining room turning the key in the lock behind her.

In the kitchen, the old lady was putting away her shopping: flour, potatoes, several bags from the green grocer, and a bulky parcel wrapped in brown paper.

'Hello, child,' Mrs Heksen's lilting voice called to her. 'Come and have a cup of tea with me.'

'Tea would be lovely.' Gee was half way through the kitchen door when she realised she was still holding the little book. She slid it down the back of her jeans, pulling her sweater over the top.

Mrs Heksen unwrapped the brown paper parcel and arranged its contents in a line on the kitchen table. 'All my best kitchen knives have been sharpened. See how they shine now.' Tenderly she touched each one in order: from a small paring knife to a ham slicer, lingering over the meat cleaver at the end of the row. 'I have a very important meal to prepare next week.'

'What's that?'

'It is a special celebration. A dinner we hold once a year, my old friends from Norway and me. This year my house has been chosen. It is a great honour.'

'Could I help?'

'Oh no. No. We do not allow outsiders. We are like a secret society of ... of cooks.'

At two o'clock the next morning Gee slid out from under Han's sturdy arm, reflecting that he'd never been a snorer until he started piling on the pounds. Earlier, she'd tried to explain the seriousness of Han's weight gain and the impact on his rugby career to Mrs Heksen as they shared a pot of tea and nibbled around the edges of their shortbread fingers. The old lady had nodded, smiled, agreed with her and they'd arranged to cook together the next day. Yet Gee felt somehow unsettled, as though nothing had really been resolved. She kissed Han's muscular back and went to make a hot drink.

GINGERBREAD

Mrs Heksen's little book was tucked away in the cupboard with the mugs where Gee had stuffed it out of sight. As she waited for the kettle to boil, she flicked through the pages, wondering how she was going to sneak it back and whether the old lady had already noticed its absence. It was cold in the kitchen, so she took the book and her mug back to the warm darkness of the bed-sitting room and curled up under a rug on the latte leather chair. Then she opened her laptop.

The online translator confirmed that 'gryte' was the Norwegian word for 'stew'. She tried a few others: 'polse' translated as 'sausage'; 'kalkum' as 'turkey'; 'risted' as 'roasted'. Gee's stomach rumbled and she fetched the biscuit tin from its hiding place in her side of the wardrobe. Cramming a chocolate dipped brandy snap into her mouth, she typed in another word: 'menneske' and the translation appeared: 'human being'. Gee checked the little book. The word was definitely 'menneske'. She checked the context: 'menneske gryte'. On the next page: 'risted menneske'. Her mouth full of brandy snap, Gee ran to the bathroom and vomited in the sink.

She crept back to the laptop and typed in 'Heksen'. And the online translator answered: 'Witch'. Gee sat perfectly still for a long time, the only wakeful person in the gingerbread house. Then she turned again to the cold glow of the laptop screen and typed 'tysbast'.

GINGERBREAD

It was still very early in the morning and the rest of the gingerbread house slept on. Nobody saw Gee pacing at the bottom of the garden, or the glint of the scissors in her hand as the sky began to lighten. Nobody saw the bright red berries she stuffed into a little bag. And nobody heard the rustle of the velvet curtain at the top of the kitchen stairs and the clatter as a pair of horn-rimmed spectacles fell from Gee's trembling fingers and down to the basement below.

'Let's make gingerbread,' Gee said the next morning as she wiped down Mrs Heksen's kitchen table. 'But with a twist. It's for my colleague, Fleur Taylor and she really loves cranberries. Could we mix in some chopped cranberries?'

'An interesting idea... I think it might... but... tch...' Mrs Heksen was distracted, searching in the drawers of the pine dresser, the kitchen cupboard, and feeling again and again in the pocket of her apron.

'Have you lost something?'

The old lady turned to Gee. 'My spectacles. I do not see so well.' She checked her pocket again. 'I must find them. I have the special meal to prepare.'

'Will you be using the recipes in that little Norwegian book?'

'Yes,' the old lady's curranty eyes shrivelled out of focus. 'Perhaps one day I will teach you.'

GINGERBREAD

'I'll help you find your glasses. But let's make the stars first.' Gee held out a little tub. 'I've already chopped the cranberries.'

Half an hour later, Han popped his head around the door.

'Ah, come in, young man,' Mrs Heksen beckoned him into the kitchen. 'Here is something delicious. And it is the creation of your own fiancée.'

'Oh no,' Gee headed him off. 'Remember your diet.'

The old lady frowned, 'Diets! I do not approve of diets. Would you have this fine young man all skin and bone? Have some now, Han, while it is warm from the oven.'

Gee replied gently but firmly. 'He will, Mrs Heksen, but first he has to earn it.' She kissed Han's cheek. 'Run down to the High Street and get the Sunday papers. The gingerbread will still be warm when you get back.'

But by the time Han returned, Mrs Heksen had been taken ill. He carried the old lady up to bed while Gee fetched a bottle of bright red liquid from the kitchen.

'It's an emetic,' she told him, sending him back downstairs. 'Mrs Heksen makes it from berries in her garden.'

By the time they called for an ambulance, it was all over.

GINGERBREAD

The inquest revealed extensive damage to a very elderly liver. Gee gave evidence concerning the tysbast bush in Mrs Heksen's garden, the old lady's frequent gathering of the berries, and the homemade emetic she had found in the larder. She also testified that Mrs Heksen had lost her horn-rimmed spectacles and Han told the hearing how he found them that afternoon in the garden. The inquest concluded 'death by misadventure' with the coroner solemnly emphasising the danger of old-wives remedies and the importance of correctly identifying plants to be used for cooking.

At somebody's suggestion, it may have been Han's or perhaps it was Gee's, the couple went away to a country house hotel in the Highlands of Scotland to recover from the shock. So nobody saw twelve elderly Norwegian women walking down the lane one dark January night, waiting on the red flag-stoned steps, salivating for their special feast. Nobody heard them hammering on the dark chocolate door, cursing the very bricks of the gingerbread house. Leaving at last with bile in their stomachs and bitterness in their hearts.

And so Gee's glittering, gilded future all began with the house.

The first series of *Gee's Gingerbread House* was a hit with viewers and critics alike. A number of spin-offs followed, including a Saturday morning magazine show also starring Han who roped in his fellow sportsmen, who in turn invited their celebrity friends. By the time Han's waistline squeezed him out of professional rugby he was already established as a media presence.

These days Gee is a global brand. Her face is everywhere: supermarkets, book stores, women's magazines, home-style magazines, cookery magazines – and still the occasional lads' mag. Mini *Gingerbread House* kiosks waft their sugary aroma throughout shopping centres across the western world, with a few scattered around China and the Middle East. Gee's themed cookery parties are very popular and every middle-class school girl across the home-counties possesses an apron, bowl and spatula set tastefully emblazoned with the *Gingerbread House* logo.

In her many interviews, Gee always acknowledges her debt to Mrs Heksen.

'Without her *Gee's Gingerbread House* simply wouldn't exist,' she insists, wiping away a tear. 'Mrs Heksen didn't just teach me to cook. She bequeathed a little of her own special magic.'

In fact the old lady bequeathed rather more than that:

'I name Gretel Geoffrey my sole heir. Gretel, my child, I have known you for only a short while, but I feel you to be the daughter I never had. You will, in time, inherit more than merely my worldly possessions.'

'That's great. We can stay on.' Han took the good fortune in his stride. 'But how did she know your name was Gretel? You never let anyone call you that.'

GINGERBREAD

Han and Gee still live in the gingerbread house; although they could easily afford something grander, Gee feels an attachment to the place. And although she might have expected her conscience to trouble her, it doesn't. If she awakes in the middle of the night to visions of vomited blood and chopped berries, she has only to go downstairs and look at the meat cleaver and the array of knives neatly arranged in the kitchen drawer. If she dreams she is holding the old lady's frail body, looking into her knowing eyes, cramming gingerbread stars into her gaping mouth and washing them down with that vile red potion, Gee clings to her handsome, increasingly portly, husband snoring in the bed beside her and whispers, 'I did it for us, Babe.'

Besides, Gee has the satisfaction of knowing she has brought good fortune and prosperity to so many. Sometimes she feels as though she's feeding the world: with food, with fun, with jobs and with dividends. Yet the sweet treats that made her fortune no longer appeal. Gee eats less and less: picking at her food, nibbling around the edges. But inside, she is always hungry, and that hunger disturbs her sleep.

One night, she leaves Han asleep in bed and wanders through the gingerbread house. Almost everything has been renovated or redecorated in some way. The stained bedroom carpet was the first to go. The dining room has been stripped out and refurnished in lighter shades; but it still has a strange

GINGERBREAD

smell, which Han doesn't seem to notice, but Gee finds unsettling. The kitchen has been updated too with modern conveniences, but it retains the charm of that sunny room where Gee and Han first tasted Mrs Heksen's gingerbread stars.

Gee stands alone in the moonlit kitchen, stroking the pine table, running her fingers along the spines of the books. Then she slips behind the velvet curtain, down the twisting stairs into the basement. To the cupboard where the little book with the red spine is still tucked away behind the mugs. Gee flicks through its pages and her hunger grows.

In the morning she will advertise for a tenant.

Incident at the Copper Kettle Tea Rooms

Monument Square was sticky with young mothers and their offspring. Each grubby little mouth gumming at a biscuit on a red and white candy-striped stick as the children splashed up the sunshine in the early April puddles. A small boy in fire-engine wellies hopped along behind a smaller girl in a fairy-princess frock, following-the-leader along the parallel lines of the new block paving (the Council's latest attempt to revitalise Rudley's town centre). They looped the loop around a middle-aged business man in a grey pin-striped suit, before crashing into one of the tables outside the Copper Kettle Tea Rooms.

INCIDENT AT THE COPPER KETTLE TEA ROOMS

Pearl looked out from the window and tried again, tried harder again, to feel any kind of connection with their world.

A young mother in faded low-rise jeans and a bright coral t-shirt stopped mid-conversation, nudged at her friend in the emerald leather jacket, and pointed. Soon all the mothers were watching Pearl watching them. She sighed and turned back to her own customers: old Mr Oliphant, his moustache dripping with tepid tea, a crust of long cold teacake in his long cold fingers; the Misses Jones and Johnson sharing a cafetiere and an iced slice; and sour Mr Pettiman, barricaded behind his Daily Express from the feeble observations of his feeble, wheelchair-bound wife. Grey hair above grey faces in beige clothes sitting at beige tables: a sepia echo of Pearl's mother, Blanche, and her companions in the day room at Sunset Lodge. Pearl towered above them like an accessorised undertaker in her customary black trousers and tunic, her matronly bosom embellished with a single blob of colour in the form of a large purple brooch.

'Aw, look at the little cuties playing in the sunshine,' eighteen-year old Rosie cooed from behind the counter. Lovely, young Rosie, the tea rooms' very own borrowed ray of sunlight, bright and shiny as the array of kettles on the shelf above her head, earning a little easy money by smiling at the old folk while she waited for a real job. Pearl, who could have made three of pretty, lissom Rosie, was aware that the girl included her among those old folk, even though her fiftieth birthday was still a couple of years away. Rosie caught her employer's eye and broadened her smile; Pearl sighed again.

Miss Jones or Miss Johnson was gazing at the children in the square. 'Why don't the kiddies come in anymore? They used to brighten the place up.'

Her companion wiped icing from her thin, lipsticked mouth. 'It's since that Gingerbread place opened.' She gave Pearl a sympathetic smile. 'You'll have lost custom there. And that smart new cafe on the High Street, the one that does fancy coffees.'

Old Mr Oliphant croaked up, 'It's quieter without them.'

'Besides,' said Miss Johnson or Miss Jones. 'You've always got us regulars. You keep things just like they've always been and you'll keep us coming back.'

Monument Square was an entry level example of 1960s commercial construction: uniform, concrete shops built around an old concrete obelisk commemorating Rudley's fallen from the first and second world wars. The Copper Kettle Tea Rooms, the sole remaining enterprise from the early days, had changed only subtly over the past fifty years. It sat between the Lavender and Lace Gift Shop and Monument Books, opposite Felicity's Florist and Al's Fruit and Veg. The other units were taken up by well known franchises, including the newest arrival, Gee's

INCIDENT AT THE COPPER KETTLE TEA ROOMS

Gingerbread, a brightly coloured plastic kiosk selling biscuits and takeaway drinks. At the back of the square, just inside the alleyway that led to Rudley's only car park, was the peeling facade of Prehistoric Pete's Rock Shop.

Pete sat at the back of his under-lit shop, among lumps of dusty stone and shining, polished crystals, and heard the children playing in the square. It must be nearly eleven, he thought, time for coffee. He swept the pile of ammonites he'd been working on from the countertop into a little basket, brushing the residue onto the floor. Then he placed the basket on a shelf between a fossilised iguanodon footprint and a section of spinosaurus jawbone, pulled a bunch of keys from the pocket of his frayed combats and ambled out into the sunshine.

A little boy in fire-engine wellies ran into Pete's legs. The boy was shorter than the legs. Pete looked down and smiled as the child looked up, then turned and ran back to his mother. A new little girl, one Pete hadn't seen before, a girl in a shiny dress, stood a few feet away and stared.

'You're very tall,' the girl announced.

'Yes I am,' Pete agreed. 'I'm six foot six.'

'You're taller than my daddy. And hairier.'

'Probably.'

'And you've got a very pointy nose.'

'Come away, Ellie-Sue,' called the girl's mother, a short young woman with thin blonde hair in two thin plaits.

INCIDENT AT THE COPPER KETTLE TEA ROOMS

'It's only Prehistoric Pete,' another mother laughed. 'He's weird, but harmless.'

Pete waved, but nobody waved back. Weird, but harmless, he thought, opening the door to the Copper Kettle Tea Rooms.

The pretty girl was clearing tables and the new owner, the big-boned woman with soft brown eyes and nice hair, was behind the counter wrapping cutlery in paper serviettes.

Pearl suppressed a groan as the tall, beaky man from the shop next door ambled in. Thin as a stick and as scruffy as his dark, disorganised shop – fraying granddad shirt, sagging trousers, sandals (even with all those puddles outside), and as for that hair and the beard ... the man looked like an off-duty wizard who'd fallen on hard times. Rosie was clearing tables so she would have to serve him herself. Pearl assumed her most discouraging look developed over twenty-five years as secretary to a local, old-school solicitor.

'Beautiful morning,' said the man, apparently not noticing the look.

'Very pleasant. What can I get you?'

'A filter coffee and, um ... let's see,' he examined the display under glass below the counter. 'A jam doughnut? Apple turnover? No ... I'll have one of your delicious pasties, please. I haven't had breakfast this morning.'

INCIDENT AT THE COPPER KETTLE TEA ROOMS

He paused, as though waiting for a reply. Then added, 'that's a lovely piece of amethyst you're wearing.'

Pearl lifted the pasty with a pair of tongs. She could feel the man watching as she popped it onto a plate, so she looked past him. The mothers were still in the square outside, the one in the coral t-shirt watching the Copper Kettle more intently than she was watching her own child. Pearl's hands began shaking as she poured the coffee and placed it on a tray beside the pasty.

'Don't be nervous,' the man smiled holding out a five pound note. 'I may be weird, but apparently I'm harmless.'

'Pardon?' Pearl looked at him.

'Or so the local mums told me.'

Rosie hurried over, bubbling with warmth and chattiness. 'We're not speaking to them,' she confided. 'They've boycotted us.'

'Boycotted?'

'Yes,' Rosie continued, oblivious to her employer's glared disapproval. 'Pearl told the kids off for playing Tig around the tables.'

'I merely told them it wasn't safe for the children to run about where people are carrying hot drinks and trays of food,' Pearl interjected, then turned away to fill a stainless steel pot with cutlery wrapped in serviettes.

'And she told them they couldn't eat those gingerbread lollies on the premises.'

INCIDENT AT THE COPPER KETTLE TEA ROOMS

'We sell our own cakes and biscuits if they want something sweet.' The pot of cutlery slipped from Pearl's fingers and spilled across the floor.

'Oops a daisy!' Rosie carried on talking. 'Anyway, the mums got all arsey and said they'd take their business elsewhere and they've been out there ever since.' The girl lowered her voice to a sinister whisper. 'Staring in at us.'

'Rosie...'

'It's not Pearl's fault. She's from a different generation. Mums are much more relaxed these days.'

'Rosie – ' Pearl could feel the heat of her reddening cheeks and neck.

'Besides, you never had children, did you Pearl? So you don't really understa – '

'Rosie!' Pearl turned her face away. 'Would you please clean this mess up before the lunchtime rush.'

Pete took his tray into the sunshine and sat down at a table in front of the window where he could see the mums chatting and laughing, and the children skipping and squealing around the square. He emptied three little packets of brown sugar into his cup, sipping the sweet black coffee as he ate his pasty with a knife and fork. He glimpsed his own reflection in the Copper Kettle's window – gaunt and grey, older than he felt. Beyond that, if he peered further in, he could see the familiar forms of the regulars stooped over their usual tables and, in the background, the woman with the nice hair wiping her eyes with a handkerchief, which she folded and tucked in her pocket.

Pete had been away when she took over. At least twice a year, he left the shop in the charge of a cash-strapped palaeontology student and headed off to some remote desert or mountain range for a month or so. Then he'd return with crates of rocks and fossils destined for museums or universities or private collectors – Pete had plenty of loyal customers. The rest of the booty he unpacked and put on display in the crowded little shop that was more of a home than the one bedroom flat where he returned to sleep at night.

Pete's phone rang. He let it ring until he finished his mouthful of pasty, then took a sip of coffee and checked the missed number: the Natural History Museum, his favourite place in the civilised world and the home of his childhood protector, the enormous diplodocus in the Dinosaur Gallery. The museum had been a sanctuary for Pete and his mother. He could never have imagined his father, a man bursting with noise and passion and the greedy imperatives of life, in that peaceful cathedral to reason and rational thought.

He pressed a couple of buttons on the phone and was soon talking to an old friend.

'George? I'll bring the mosasaur vertebrae down at the weekend.'

As they chatted, Pete gazed back through the window at the woman inside briskly setting tables

INCIDENT AT THE COPPER KETTLE TEA ROOMS

ready for the lunchtime diners. He wondered how many others had taken their custom elsewhere, paying over the odds for the superficial bonhomie the tea rooms' new owner was so ill equipped to provide. So, her name was Pearl ... pearls for tears. Well, Pete had just the thing for that. He picked up two little red and white sticks from under the table, counted out a tip, and ambled back to his shop, dropping the rubbish in a bin as he passed.

Pearl watched from behind the counter as the last of the lunchtime diners scraped up their custard and apple pie. She could hear Rosie in the kitchen singing something sickly about love as she loaded the dishwasher. Pearl turned up the volume on her CD of classical music.

Although the mothers had taken their offspring home for lunch, they were still all too present in Pearl's thoughts. Did those silly women really want their children scalded by hot tea, or cut by broken china? Was it so unreasonable of Pearl to ask them not to eat that wretched gingerbread in her tea rooms?

Pearl recollected an angular woman with an indomitable air, clad in a brown dress and starched white apron serving tea and fancy cakes to well behaved customers, including a nine-year-old Pearl and her parents. Mrs Sharp, proprietress of the Copper Kettle Tea Rooms from its inception to her death in service in 1991, would have had no truck with modern mothers. Her customers had known their place – and it wasn't always in the right.

Yet Pearl remembered the place with fondness, a cosy haven after a day out walking with Mum and Dad. The tea rooms had seemed a sensible investment of her redundancy money. It was like Mum always said: 'Don't dream too big, my girl – big dreams grow into big nightmares.' Anyone else would just have said, 'Be careful what you wish for', but Pearl's Mum always liked to ram her message home with an alarming metaphor. At least she had until last spring, a year ago on Sunday, when the stroke had stopped her voice. Maybe Mum had dreamed of a peaceful old age and Sunset Lodge was the nightmare she got instead – so peaceful she might as well have died.

Pearl was accustomed to small, sensible dreams within the limitations imposed by society on a big-boned girl with an old-fashioned name. She'd never challenged those limitations; never hung out in the town centre with Shaz, Caz and Trisha; never been so busy snogging Steve or Kev she'd missed the last bus home. And Mum was always there to make sure Pearl wasn't at a loose end: Monday nights down at the church hall helping with the teas for the Ladies' Guild; Tuesdays and Thursdays at the dining room table working on correspondence courses in shorthand and typing. Pearl's favourite day of the week was Saturday when she accompanied Dad to the local

INCIDENT AT THE COPPER KETTLE TEA ROOMS

cricket club and was sometimes allowed to join in the practice sessions.

'That girl of yours could have bowled for the county,' the club chairman told Dad with a sigh. 'Ah, she'd have made a strapping boy.'

As for Pearl, she never complained that she wasn't a boy, or one of the popular girls at school. Or that the only clothes available from Mum's catalogue made her look forty years old and the name her parents had chosen for her made her sound sixty.

'We'd waited so long for a child,' Mum used to say, 'and you were like a beautiful little pearl in my hands.' Then she'd add, 'Now you're more like a giant clam – you could swallow up your Dad and me.'

Which was true. By the time she left school, strapping young Pearl towered over her dainty, old-fashioned parents.

When Pearl went to work for Blunt, Partridge and Stevens, she felt she fitted in for the first time in her life. Old Mr Blunt appreciated steadiness and efficiency and, in a job that combined the roles of secretary and portcullis, Pearl's demeanour was an asset at last. She also discovered sex, and that certain men liked a big-boned girl with a no-nonsense manner, especially if they could call her 'Nanny' or 'Ma'am'. But, after a handful of less than romantic encounters, Pearl opted for the single life.

Blunt, Partridge and Stevens proved such a comfortable rut that twenty-five years slipped by barely noticed. Until the day old Mr Blunt was finally persuaded to retire and Pearl was stripped out along with the rest of his archaic office furniture. Still, the severance package had been generous – hence the purchase of the Copper Kettle Tea Rooms.

It had seemed such a modest venture; a dream even Mum would approve of. Not like sailing a felucca down the Nile, or galloping bareback through the Grand Canyon. Not like running away with the gypsies. It wasn't a big dream at all – not adventure, or love, or a family of her own – but it had certainly been a big mistake. No matter, Pearl told herself firmly, it was a mistake that was easy to rectify. She reached under the counter for a white envelope embossed with a little red gingerbread house.

'Rosie,' she called through to the kitchen, 'would you come and hold the fort? I need to make a few phone calls.'

Pete wandered in around three o'clock. Most of the tables were empty and there was no sign of Pearl. He ordered a pot of tea and a hot cross bun.

'By way of lunch,' he explained.

Rosie laughed lightly and gave a good show of listening. 'I'm all on my own. Pearl's gone out.'

'Oh?'

'Yes. All very sudden and very hush-hush,' the girl adopted her sinister stage-whisper and Pete noticed the handful of customers shift in their seats, inclining their hearing aids in her direction. 'I heard her on the phone after lunch. She's gone to see her solicitor.' Then in her normal voice, 'I'll bring your bun over when it's ready.'

Pete took his tea outside, put the tray on a table near the window and sat down. He winced, stood up, and took a round piece of blackened rock, the size of a tennis ball, from the front pocket of his combats, placing it on the table. Dust settled on the shiny metal surface, and Pete settled in his chair. He squashed the teabag inside the teapot, selected three sachets of white sugar and emptied them into his cup. By the time Rosie appeared with his hot cross bun and pats of butter, Pete was sipping his tea and reading *The Geological Society Periodical*.

'Oh, isn't it lovely out here in the sunshine. The puddles have nearly dried up,' Rosie trilled. She looked over Pete's shoulder. 'Your magazine looks heavy going!'

'It's full of the earth's treasures.'

'What? Like this bit of old coal.'

'Ah. This one has a hidden secret,' Pete smiled, picking up the rock. 'It might look dull on the outside, but ... let me show you ...'

Rosie glanced across the square. 'Better not,' she said. 'Here comes Pearl.'

Pearl walked into Monument Square just as the mothers and toddlers arrived back, their ranks swollen by siblings from the local primary school. She spotted the emerald jacket and the coral t-shirt

INCIDENT AT THE COPPER KETTLE TEA ROOMS

and straightened her spine, glad for once that she stood a good six foot two, even in low heels. As she crossed the square, Pearl closed her ears to the mothers' muttered remarks, pretending not to see their children pulling faces. The pin-striped business man was back, stubbing out his cigarette on the block paving. Pearl opened her mouth to chastise him, but the man turned away to stare at the window display in Felicity's Florist. Outside the Copper Kettle Tea Rooms, Rosie was chatting to the tall, scruffy man – not, Pearl thought, a very good advert for the establishment.

As her employer approached, Rosie hurried back inside. Pearl was almost at the door when the man spoke.

'We haven't been formally introduced,' he said, 'so I'll do the honours. I'm Pete, commonly known as Prehistoric Pete. And you,' he added, giving her no chance to ignore him, 'are Pearl. Pleased to meet you.'

'Delighted,' Pearl replied, without meeting his gaze.

'I don't think you are,' the man replied gently. 'You don't know me and you probably think I'm as peculiar as they do.' He indicated the mothers and children queuing for gingerbread and coffee. 'I don't know you either, but I think you have beautiful eyes and you look very sad today.'

INCIDENT AT THE COPPER KETTLE TEA ROOMS

Pearl was preparing her portcullis glare when she heard laughter from across the square and looked down.

'Don't mind them,' said Prehistoric Pete, standing and holding out a chair. 'Sit down here and drink a cup of tea with me.'

He called through to Rosie. 'Another tea, please.'

Protesting, but weakly, Pearl sat.

'So now I'm supposed to tell you all my troubles?' she mumbled as she fiddled with the packets of sugar.

'Absolutely not. Why would you? We've only just been introduced.'

Pearl looked past the scruffy, grey facial hair and noticed Pete's eyes were the colour of amber and that under his long thin beak of a nose was a surprisingly kind smile.

Pete watched as Pearl added a single sweetener to her tea.

'Those women,' he indicated across the square, 'do they really bother you?'

'Yes,' Pearl admitted. 'But mainly because they make me realise what a mistake it was to buy the Copper Kettle. I'm not really a people person.'

'Not really,' Pete agreed.

Pearl gave a little frown.

'I'm not sure I am either,' he confessed. 'I much prefer fossils. I quite like people, but I've never found it easy to rub along smoothly with them. Too weird, I suppose.'

'But harmless,' Pearl corrected with a smile. 'Anyway, it doesn't really matter now. I'm selling up. I can't do this and I've had a very good offer.'

'What about your regulars?'

'They're not really *my* regulars. I'm afraid they'll just have to develop a taste for gingerbread.' She pulled a little red and white spike out from under Pete's tray.

'Ah, those ubiquitous plastic sticks.'

Pearl nodded. 'They're looking for bigger premises to host parties and pop-in-and-bake sessions. I suppose mothers don't want the mess at home anymore.'

She picked up the round rock and Pete noticed black dust all over the table.

'My father hated mess,' he mumbled, brushing it away with his sleeve. 'Used to drive him mad.' Dust stuck to his shirt and a little fell onto Pearl's lap where it nestled in the folds of her black tunic.

Pearl put the rock down. 'What is it?'

'A geode. They're very interesting – hidden secrets. But,' Pete felt in his shirt pocket, 'this is what I really wanted you to see.'

He held out a polished, brownish-black stone, the size of a plump acorn, and waited for Pearl to take it.

'Obsidian. Hold it up to the light, it's translucent.' Pete watched as she examined the stone, peering at it in the bright sunlight. He hesitated, drawing on a bit of courage. 'It's for you.'

Pearl lowered her arm. 'What? Why ... I don't really...'

'Please. There's a reason. A legend.' He waited until she turned her face to look at him. 'It's also called an Apache tear. Back in 1870 the US cavalry trapped a group of Pinal Apaches up on Big Picacho – it's in Arizona. Most of the braves were slaughtered, but the rest, the last twenty five, rode their horses off the cliff top rather than be killed by the soldiers.' Pete paused until Pearl gestured for him to carry on. 'The Apache women and children gathered on the white sand near to the foot of the cliffs to grieve for their menfolk. After they had wept for a whole moon's cycle the gods turned their tears into black obsidian stones, embedded in the white sand.'

Pete reached out and gently raised Pearl's hand back up to the light. 'Look now and you can see the tear inside. The legend says if you own an Apache tear you need never cry again, because the Apache women have already wept for you.'

He saw that Pearl's eyes were shining, but not with tears.

'Thank you,' she spoke so softly Pete leaned closer to catch her words.

Then he heard a harsher noise, a wolf whistle from one of the mothers, followed by communal cackling as the others turned to look.

INCIDENT AT THE COPPER KETTLE TEA ROOMS

Pete felt Pearl pull her hand away and heard the scrape of her chair against the block paving. He was about to speak when she snatched up the geode and hurled it across the square.

The mothers screamed and scattered, gathering up their children as they ran. The geode missed them all. But it hit its mark, a respectable looking business man in a grey pinstriped suit, smack on the back of his head. And as he fell the man let go of a little boy in fire engine wellies who tottered, crying, back to his mother, the woman in the coral t-shirt and low-rise jeans.

Pearl locked the door behind the last of the mothers and hung up a little sign that read 'The Copper Kettle Tea Rooms will be pleased to serve you again at 8.00am'. Then she closed the window blinds and sank down at a table for two with her head in her hands.

Rosie brought her a cup of tea. 'For our local heroine,' she announced. 'You'll be all over the papers tomorrow.'

Pearl visualised the article 'Pearl Bowls a Paedo Over!', accompanied by a picture of herself and the mothers – a sour middle-aged raven surrounded by a flock of simpering birds of paradise. 'I hope not,' she replied without looking up.

'Really?' the girl sounded disappointed. 'It'll be great publicity. Not that you'll need it now all the mums and kids are coming back. We'll be heaving!'

INCIDENT AT THE COPPER KETTLE TEA ROOMS

'There's something I need tell you,' Pearl began, but when she looked up Rosie had disappeared into the kitchen. 'It can wait till tomorrow,' she added to herself.

Pearl sent Rosie home and did the clearing up alone, stacking and wiping and hoovering in silence. By the time she had finished, all the shops in Monument Square were in darkness and the street lights were coming on. It was after seven; too late to drive over to Sunset Lodge to visit Mum, thank goodness. Yes, it would be lonely at home, but it was her mother she wanted, not that slack-faced stranger. Actually, it was Dad she really wanted, even after twenty years, his small but solid presence a blueprint of the companionship she might have dreamed of. Pearl reached into her pocket for a hanky and found the Apache tear.

She locked up and turned into the alleyway. There was still a light in Prehistoric Pete's Rock Shop. Pearl stopped outside and knocked on the door.

Pete scrubbed at the insides of his two least chipped beakers with a little brush normally used for cleaning fossils, aware of Pearl pretending not to notice. He used an attachment on his penknife to open a bottle of Claret. Feeling shy and dusty, he took one of the beakers to Pearl who was perched on a wonky wooden stool amidst half-unpacked crates and overcrowded displays of fossils, crystals and other pieces of stone.

'I'm sorry I broke your rock,' she said.

'My rock?'

'The ... geode did you call it?' Pearl sipped her wine. 'It broke when it hit that man. I'm sorry.'

'It doesn't matter. I was going to break it open anyway. I told you, they have hidden secrets. Look.'

Pete took a lump of round black rock from one of the crates. He put it on the counter and tapped it with a little hammer and chisel until it split in two. Then he held the rock out to Pearl, watching her face as he broke the two pieces apart, enjoying her surprise at the sparkling crystals within.

'Not a very promising exterior. But inside each one is a little crystal cave: white, blue, pink. Some of the finest examples are amethyst cathedrals.' Pete flicked a switch to illuminate a display case of large hollowed rocks glittering with purple crystals. 'Amethyst – like your brooch.'

Encouraged by Pearl's smile, he continued, 'It's a lovely colour on you. Really suits you ... Pearl, why do you wear so much black?'

'Mum said I should. Because it's slimming.'

Pete looked down at his own scrawny frame and laughed. 'Could she recommend a fattening colour for me?'

Monument Square was quiet and peaceful in the darkness; deserted but for two tall figures saying goodnight.

INCIDENT AT THE COPPER KETTLE TEA ROOMS

'Will you be in for coffee tomorrow morning?' Pearl asked. 'It would be good to see a friendly face after I've broken the news to Rosie and the regulars.'

'I'll be in,' Pete replied. 'But are you still going to sell? Now that everyone loves you?'

'Ah, but I don't love them. I don't imagine I ever could.'

The figures reached out and shook hands awkwardly, then made a brief, clumsy embrace.

'What will you do instead?'

'I'd like to travel. Maybe to see where those geodes and my Apache tear came from. Mum won't miss me. She doesn't even know me anymore. I've always wanted to travel, it just seemed too ...'

Pearl's voice faltered, but the warmth of Pete's smile filled her with courage and she began again with new strength. 'However, I think, since even the smallest of dreams can become a nightmare ... well then, from now on I shall allow myself bigger dreams.'

The Wish Child

A lady writer come... came, I mean... today. They got us all together in the day room — the walking dead and us ones on wheels. I got parked between Doreen who always wees on the floor and that old chap with the bow tie who shouts out things: 'Good morning, my dear' and 'Bleep off out of it, you bleeping bleep'. They put me there 'cos I never complain.

This writer woman. Shortlisted for something or other. Well I'd never heard of her. And I didn't think much of her stories, neither. You know them stories where nothing much happens and then the main character dies at the end. Still, someone must want to buy 'em — she had a posh enough dress on. Didn't mean 'them stories' I meant 'those stories'. My grammar's gone to pot these days. I sound worse than me mum.

Lucky Arthur's not here to hear me. Not that anybody can hear me anyway.

They was trying to get us to talk about our own lives. Tell our own stories. Not me, of course. Nobody expects me to say anything. This last year, they don't think I've got nothing ... anything ... to say. That new one – the thin girl with bad skin – she held my hand and said, 'I bet you could tell us a story, Blanche. I bet you've seen a thing or two in your life.' I don't like it when they call you by your first name. The familiarity. I never said they could call me Blanche, but they all do. Still, she's a kind girl that one. Homely, but kind.

And I could tell them a story. I might be wearing elasticated slacks and a stained jumper, but I could tell a better one than that soppy woman for all her smart clothes. I know a corker of a story, a proper old fashioned fireside tale like folk used to tell. I'll tell you it now. Are you sitting comfortably?

A brave little peasant woman lived with her husband in a small stone cottage on the edge of an enchanted wood. They lived quietly in peace with their neighbours and they kept themselves to themselves.

The woman loved her husband dearly, as he loved her. She was a beauty in miniature with shining, golden hair that curled round her pretty face. He was scarcely taller, but fine looking and strong, a mantelpiece Galahad. The couple were well matched in temperament, as in height. Childhood sweethearts who in all their years of marriage spoke hardly an angry word. But there was a sorrow in their hearts and an emptiness. The couple never spoke of this.

for they feared their words would feed the emptiness until it filled the little stone cottage and spilled into the world outside, dragging their love away with it.

The secret sorrow lived unseen between them. From time to time the wife would glimpse it in the middle of the night, nestling at the foot of the bed where a cot might have stood. Or the husband would stare a while at the apple tree outside the kitchen window, the one with the strong, straight bough, fashioned by God especially for a child's swing. And every time she stirred the Christmas pudding, or knelt in church, or visited a wishing well, the brave little peasant woman would make a silent wish.

Years went by slowly, quietly, until, on a morning exactly twenty-five years from the day they had made their marriage vows, the husband presented his wife with a silver bangle. It was as delicate and shining as she herself, an ornament any fine lady would be proud to wear.

'It must have cost the earth,' she exclaimed in wonder.

'You are all the earth to me,' her husband replied. And, being a man of few words, he said no more.

The little peasant woman kept this moment in her heart and whenever she thought of her secret sorrow she would stroke the bangle, remember his words, and feel some comfort.

THE WISH CHILD

The small stone cottage stood on the outskirts of a village, but the little peasant woman preferred to do her marketing in the town that lay on the other side of the enchanted wood. In the town, the eggs were larger, the flour more finely ground, and she could gaze into the windows of the fancy shops and dream a little.

The shortest way to town was by a path that led through the middle of the wood, but the local people preferred the longer road that skirted around the edge. On one side of this road lay open pasture, on the other leafy green trees with strong straight trunks and branches where birds gathered to sing in the sunlight. But beyond those trees, the wood grew close, dark and twisted, and the creatures that lived there grew the same. So, when the brave little peasant woman set off for town one spring morning, she kept to the road.

It was a beautiful morning, the grass shining with daisies and buttercups, the trees and hedgerows heavy with white blossom. The air was ringing with birdsong and the little peasant woman swung her basket as she strode along. When she was halfway to the town, she heard the sound of voices among the trees and turned to see a group of gypsy caravans set back from the road and three dark-haired, dark-eyed children pinning up tattered posters. Crow black words on a crimson background:

THE WISH CHILD

FOR ONE NIGHT ONLY
THE TRAVELLING FAIR
AMUSEMENTS,
AMAZEMENTS,
FORTUNES TOLD

The little peasant woman set down her basket and stood a while watching, until she became aware that she too was being watched. Beside a caravan a man stood tearing a roasted chicken between his teeth. He was a hulk of a man, dressed all in black with an old red kerchief at his neck, young and strong, tall and broad as a half-bred giant. An old woman was seated up on the caravan steps. She was dark as the shadow he cast over her, a stunted, bundled-up thing in an old red dress and shawl, her face half hidden beneath black lace. In her lap lay a shining crystal ball. The peasant woman stared at the fortune teller and the fortune teller stared back. Then she held aloft the crystal ball, and beckoned.

Turning her back on the gypsies, the little peasant woman picked up her basket and strode on towards the town. She bought eggs and flour and other provisions, passing the time of day with the shopkeepers. Then she stepped into her favourite store for something pretty to make a summer dress. Inside, two young mothers were admiring each other's babies. The little peasant woman smiled and wished them both 'Good afternoon', but, although she stood looking at the rolls of fabric until closing time, she left the store without buying a thing.

Pale and sad, the woman walked slowly back along the road, her basket heavy as her heart. The sky was darker now, clouds hiding the sinking sun. As she approached the place where the gypsies were camped, she lowered her head to hurry on, but the secret sorrow rose up inside her heart. Slowly, guiltily, the brave little peasant woman turned from the fading sunlight and the last of the birdsong. She looked into the trees. To the flickering red lanterns and the cawing laughter of the Travelling Fair.

'First you must cross my palm with silver.' The fortune teller's voice was as coarse and dark as the wood.

The little peasant woman dropped two coins into her hand, shrinking from the gnarled fingers and long, cruel nails painted red as blood.

The fortune teller took the woman by the wrist and drew her into the dark of the caravan.

'I know what you want me to see,' she said as she caressed the crystal ball. 'Your heart and the emptiness within.' She held the ball aloft and peered into its depths. 'I know what you wish for.'

'And do you ... What do you see?' urged the brave little peasant woman.

'I can see what you want me to see ...' the fortune teller rasped. 'If you are prepared to pay the price.'

'I would pay ... anything.'

'Then tonight, when the fair is over, you must return alone. You must walk the path through the enchanted wood.'

The little peasant woman shivered, but she nodded.

'You will reach a fork in the path. Do not turn left or right, but go straight on, into the trees, until you come to a clearing with a large flat rock. Speak your wish to the wood then lie down and sleep a night on that rock.'

'And I will have ...? I will get...?'

'You will get the thing you wish for.'

Trembling, the little peasant woman turned to go.

'Three more things,' said the fortune teller. 'Firstly, whatever happens, you must tell no one. If you tell then your wish will be taken from you.'

Eagerly, the little peasant woman nodded her agreement.

'Secondly, you must swear to speak no ill of the gypsies. If you speak evil of us, then evil will befall you and yours.'

Willingly, the little peasant woman swore to speak only fair words of the gypsy folk.

'Thirdly,' said the fortune teller, 'there is a price to pay. A price of silver.' And she pointed to the shining silver bangle around the woman's wrist.

The little peasant woman hid her arm, bangle and all, behind her back. 'But ... my husband's gift ...'

'You said you would pay anything.'

THE WISH CHILD

So what d'you think of my story so far? What about them gippos, eh? When I was a girl we knowed to steer clear ... knew, I mean. Mind you, we was fascinated by 'em too.

I went to one of them fortune tellers once. Never told Arthur. He'd have laughed and said it was all nonsense, but it weren't. It weren't no laughing matter either. Our little peasant woman knew that. You do deals with gippos and fortune tellers, you gotta pay the price. Dream big dreams and you better get ready for big nightmares.

After midnight, the brave little peasant woman rose from her bed and, careful not to wake her husband, she slipped on her clothes, wrapped herself in his warm cloak and tiptoed out of the small stone cottage and into the enchanted wood. At first the path was wide and easy, the trees set far apart, their trunks straight and true. Moonlight shone through the high branches and it was not too hard to be brave. But as she walked deeper into the wood, the trees grew closer together, their trunks twisted, wrestling for the meagre light. The path became overgrown, roots and ivy snatching at the peasant woman's feet and legs, thorns catching at her skirts. All around the undergrowth rustled with the scurrying of creatures that live in the dark, while above branches interlaced like a trap.

But the little peasant woman did not falter and when she came to the place where the path forked she walked straight on into the trees, her heart beating faster as the air grew stale and damp, and her courage grew cold.

At last she reached the clearing, and in the centre, just as the fortune teller had said, there was a large flat rock, the size of a marriage bed. The brave little peasant woman took off her silver bangle and placed it where the bed head would be. Then she lay down on the rock and covered her shivering body with her husband's cloak. As the trees wove a cage about the clearing, she spoke her wish aloud to the wood.

'I wish for a child.'

Enchantment burst through the trees. An ogre, strong as a giant. Grunting like an animal. The ogre ripped away the cloak, lifting the little peasant woman with one brutal hand. The other hand caught up her shining golden hair, twisting it cruelly. The ogre's black eyes shone with lust. Its lips dripped with the stench of old meat and ale. Filthy nails tore through her clothes. Yellow teeth bit into her flesh.

The brave little peasant woman closed her eyes, praying to God and the angels that she would survive. Closing her ears to the ogre's mocking laugh, she whispered over and over again, 'I wish for a child.'

Early the next morning, a single, redeeming sunbeam found a way through the cage of branches and gently kissed the bruised cheek of the brave little peasant woman. She opened her eyes and found herself alone on the rock, her golden hair turned to silver. Shaking with cold and fear, she dressed, wrapping her husband's cloak around her. She searched in vain for her bangle at the place where the bed head would be, and found in its place a soiled red kerchief.

Do you want to hear they all lived happy ever after? The little peasant woman's gonna get what she wanted, and the big bad ogre's gone away.

Hah! Nothing lasts for ever after. My Arthur certainly didn't and I'm nearly done for – though I'm still holding on inside, whatever they think. When I was in the hospital there was a doctor said I had this 'locked-in' syndrome. Nice boy, but he only came the once. Nobody else much bothered. They don't when you're old.

Of course I am over ninety, and I was doing pretty well till me stroke. Having my Pearl kept me young – no use moaning on about aches and pains when there's a littlun round your feet. And I had my Arthur – a man of few words maybe, but a man in a million. I always tried to be a lady for him – talk nice, act proper. But he was took that sudden. I become an old woman overnight when he died.

I used to look at Pearl and wonder where my little girl was – not that she was ever that little. Bigger than both of us by the time she reached her teens. You wish and wait so long for a little baby and then she's grown in a flash. No, there's no such thing as ever after.

Want to know what happened to the little peasant woman?

I'll tell you.

THE WISH CHILD

When the wish child was born on the first day of the New Year, the brave little peasant woman's husband said little, but he cried with joy. Their neighbours brought gifts and good wishes for the baby girl. And if anyone noticed her swarthy skin, her thick dark hair and deep black eyes, then good manners stopped their tongues.

The wish child grew tall and strong. She was a hungry baby and a demanding toddler with fierce eyes and grabbing hands, but in time her parents' patience and their peaceful ways soothed her into an obedient childhood. The sun lightened her hair to the colour of mahogany and kindness softened her eyes to a gentle chestnut. The little peasant woman made her a warm blue cloak, lined with rabbit fur, and her love for the girl grew with every day that passed.

The brave little peasant woman never set foot in the enchanted wood, nor did she allow the wish child to play in the shade of its trees. Every time she walked to the town, she peered into the shadows for a sign of the gypsies. And every spring she did her marketing in the village and listened carefully to her neighbours for news of the Travelling Fair. But the gypsies stayed away and, in time, that terrible night faded to the memory of a memory of a terrible dream.

By the time the wish child reached her thirteenth year she was growing into a comely young woman, although she lacked her mother's frail beauty. The little peasant woman was herself approaching old age, her hair more white now than silver, but the years had been kind and she was not yet bent or ailing.

That Spring there was an abundance of blossom and one afternoon the wish child danced in from school, her arms heavy with crimson flowers.

'A man gave them to me,' she laughed. 'A big, dark man dressed all in black. He looked me up and down and said he had known my mother.'

The brave little peasant woman snatched the flowers and threw them on the fire. She chose her words carefully.

'If you see that man again,' she told the child, 'do not talk to him. Come straight home to me.'

The next afternoon the wish child came running in from school, cheeks flushed and her dark eyes gleaming.

'Mama,' cried the wish child. 'There's to be a Travelling Fair tonight – on the road to town. May I go, Mama? Please?'

The brave little peasant woman took her daughter by the hand.

'No,' she said, quietly and pressed her hand to her mouth to say no more.

But the girl prattled on about fairs and painted caravans, each word another rent in her mother's resolve. Until the little peasant woman cried aloud.

'It is a heathen fair! Full of wicked folk with evil gypsy ways. Good girls stay away from such places.'

Then, her heart racing, she set the wish child enough chores to keep her busy until bedtime.

That night while her husband and her daughter slept, the brave little peasant woman sat alone downstairs in the small stone cottage. White-faced and wide-eyed, she wrapped herself in her husband's cloak and stoked the fire with kindling. The dry twigs made a cage around the dying flames.

Just after midnight, she saw a dark shape outside the window. Then she heard a heavy footfall on the path and a banging on the back door. The brave little peasant woman's heart quaked at the thought of what might be standing outside in the darkness, but it quaked more to think the noise would summon her husband or daughter from their bed. So she stood up as tall as she could and opened the door.

The ogre was standing there. Older, as she was herself, but tall and broad as her nightmares. Its eyes as black, its teeth as yellow. Swinging a bough torn from the apple tree in one of its brutal hands.

'I will come with you,' she said though her voice shook. 'But we must be quiet and not wake my husband.'

The ogre laughed and its laugh was every bit as mocking. 'I haven't come for you, old woman. Your bones are dry sticks that would snap in my fingers. Your flesh is stale and gristled.' The ogre's tongue licked around its dripping lips. 'I want strong young bones I can bend to my pleasure. I want plump young flesh that gives beneath my teeth.' It leaned closer, black eyes peering inside the cottage and, hanging around its neck, the little peasant woman saw a chain loaded with rings and trinkets, her own silver bangle dangling in the middle.

'I've come,' said the ogre, 'for what is mine.'

Have you got a child? My mum told me she didn't know fear till she had us kids. Soon as that baby starts in your belly, your heart starts peeling, layer by layer till it's raw. And your eyes become keener, opened up to all the evil in the world.

If only every child could have a guardian angel or a fairy godmother. But there's no good fairies, not in my story. In this life you have to make your own luck – and your own endings.

The brave little peasant woman looked the ogre in the eye.

'If I let you have my daughter, will you promise to leave my husband and me in peace?'

'What use would I have for you two feeble creatures? Bring me the girl.'

'I cannot fetch her now. My husband will wake.'

'Then I will rip him apart. Bring me the girl.'

'I cannot,' she stammered. 'Her cries will bring the neighbours running.'

The ogre gripped her arm in his strong, sweaty fist. 'I will have what is mine. If I have to crush you and your husband. If I have to drag her out in front of the whole village.'

The brave little peasant woman bowed her head. 'I beg you. Let me bring her to you quietly.

THE WISH CHILD

Tomorrow night – at midnight. To that place in the enchanted wood where she began.'

The ogre leered a smile as, wielding the bough that had once held a child's swing, he turned and lumbered away, leaving only the stench of liquor and violence.

The next morning the wish child found her mother asleep in a chair by the cold remains of the fire. A kitchen knife lay by her hand, the family bible open on her lap.

'Mama. Wake up, Mama,' she cried. 'I've had the strangest dreams. I dreamed I went into the enchanted wood.'

The little peasant woman rose stiffly from her chair, marking her place in the bible with the kitchen knife.

'No school today,' she said. 'I need you to help me here at home.'

As soon as her husband had gone to his work, the little peasant woman gave the wish child her first task. 'The beans need planting out. Cut me thirty long strong stakes from the saplings in the garden to support them as they grow.'

Then she set her digging. 'For the carrots. Turn the soil over well and make a pile of all the stones you find.'

When this was done, the little peasant woman gave the wish child a purse of money and sent her to the village for three bottles of ale.

THE WISH CHILD

While the girl was away, her mother took a dozen of the stakes and whittled the ends with her kitchen knife until they were sharp as spears and hid them among the trees at the edge of the enchanted wood. The rest she set aside for the beans. Then she sorted through the stones until she found one the size of her own fist. She hid the stone in her pinafore pocket along with a single long, woollen stocking.

When the wish child returned, the little peasant woman killed two chickens and brought them into the house. She closed the shutters, lit candles in the kitchen and set her daughter to plucking and preparing the birds for the pot.

'I will only be gone for an hour,' she said. 'If anyone comes knocking, do not answer the door.'

That evening, the wish child and her papa were delighted with their feast of chicken stew and ale. After they had eaten, they were full and tired and went early to their beds. Then the brave little peasant woman took the third bottle of ale from the pantry and a second pot of stew from the oven. She put them in her basket with an old red table cloth and walked again into the enchanted wood.

An hour before midnight the peasant woman returned to the small stone cottage, and tiptoed up the stairs to the wish child's bedside.

In the clearing at the heart of the enchanted wood lay a rock, large and smooth as a marriage bed. Beside the rock a tall figure clad in a blue fur-lined cloak waited, solitary as a bride. All around her the trees twisted themselves into a cage.

At midnight, the ogre crashed into the clearing, its brutal hands ready to take and tear. Then it smelled the chicken stew and ale and hesitated. The ogre peered at the figure through the darkness, at the blue fur-lined cloak and two long plaits of mahogany hair. Its lips parted with desire and its tongue slavered between yellow teeth. With a trembling hand, the figure pointed to a red cloth, stretched out like a high table and laden with food and drink.

Grunting, the ogre turned to the food, ladling chicken stew into its mouth with one hand while the other grasped the bottle of ale. With the speed of a warrior, the cloaked figure leapt down from a tree stump, whirling a long wool stocking twice in the air and bringing the rock tied within it smashing down into the back of the ogre's head. The monster turned, roaring with pain and rage. The stocking was swung again, the rock brought crashing up under its jaw. The ogre fell backwards through the table cloth onto a dozen sharpened stakes of wood.

Many dark hours later, a single early morning sunbeam found a way through the interlaced branches, down into the clearing, glinting on the rings and trinkets hanging around the dying ogre's neck. As the monster choked on its final breath, the brave little peasant woman threw off the hood of her daughter's cloak and took back her silver bangle.

Perhaps, after all, they could've lived happy ever after. Well, happy as you can when one can't sleep 'cos they've a murderer's conscience, and one can't in case someone comes in the night and cuts her hair off again. Maybe the husband was happy in his ignorance — until his heart gave up before his time.

Oh I can tell a good story. Like folk used to tell, like fairy tales and the bible before they prettied them up. David and Goliath — that was always one of my favourites. A plucky little underdog and a villain straight from hell.

My Pearl come ... came ... in earlier. She come to tell me goodbye, she's off to America of all places. Said something about the gypsy in her. Started me off crying but the tears couldn't get out. I've been holding onto me bangle since she went even though it makes me feel sad. Thinking about Arthur. Worrying about Pearl. America! God only knows what'll happen to her there. Big dreams turn to big nightmares. I wanted to shout out: Don't you go, my girl. You're asking too much, dream smaller. My precious, precious Pearl — something beautiful from something so ugly.

They'll come and put me to bed soon. I hope it's the skinny, spotty one. 'Night, night, Blanche,' she'll say as she strokes my cheek. 'Sleep well.'

Who knows, perhaps tonight I might. Perhaps tonight will bring that last, long, dreamless sleep to free me from my nightmares.

Vanessa Chesterton's Wishes

Vanessa Chesterton tells herself she has every right to be nervous. Only an imbecile, she tells herself, wouldn't be nervous on such an occasion. Here she is fraternising with the publishing elite in the ballroom of the Fortesque Hotel – her new, and very pricy, black silk trouser suit creasing if she even thinks of sitting down, while the even pricier crimson under-wired bodice pokes into Vanessa's armpits every time her posture relaxes. Stiffly she takes her place at the designated table with its shining white cloth, silver cutlery and crystal glasses. Seated with her are Vanessa's agent, her editor, and the managing director of the company that has been publishing her books for the last twenty years, all accompanied by their loyal spouses. Vanessa is not similarly encumbered; her spouse departed as soon as their children made it through puberty – thus proving himself possessed of greater staying power than her father. Instead, allowing her misgivings to be outweighed by a more pressing agenda, Vanessa has brought Essie along. And, as if there wasn't enough to feel nervous about, Essie has gone missing.

Vanessa's party are seated at one of forty gleaming circular tables, satellites to the head table up on the stage. The Diamond Nib Award is the industry's premier prize for female writers. This year the judges are joined by Ron Birch, author of *The Burning Girl*, the book that inspired the film tipped to dominate next month's Oscars. Later the chairman of judges will make a speech and their celebrity guest will present the winner with an impressive statuette of a classical figure embracing an oversized quill.

The perimeter of the ballroom is decorated with banners that hang from the gallery to the floor, banners emblazoned with the symbol of the Diamond Nib, alternated with studio shots of the nominated authors clutching their books and smiling down on the proceedings with varying degrees of confidence. Vanessa scans the other nominees, dismissing nine as also-rans. From her first reading of the short list, it was obvious there were only three serious contenders. She studies the pictures of those three. Vanessa acknowledges her own expression might seem a little too aware of being the bookies' favourite. Marietta O'Donnell looks complacent with the knowledge that she already has two Diamond Nibs on her mantelpiece, although everyone knows the judges are unlikely to award a third. Ty Floyde is characteristically enigmatic – shy yet confident, youthful yet worldly, pierced yet pretty. As Vanessa has told Essie on many occasions, whenever she sees that face she wants to slap it.

Where is Essie anyway? Perhaps she's gone to tone down her outfit. Granted the red cocktail dress is plausible, even with black leather lacing from cleavage to hem, but it clashes with her orange hair and the fetish boots are a stride too far – even for Essie. She might be sulking, Vanessa has been less than delicate with her criticism. Opening the clasp of her sequined evening bag she pretends to look for a tissue. No, Essie isn't hiding in there. Maybe she's already on the case.

'You know what you have to do?' Vanessa stood before the hall mirror, patting her newly auburn curls and wondering if a lighter shade would have edged her appearance to the right side of forty-five.

'Of course!' trilled a little voice from her evening bag. 'It will be both easy and peasy, Vanessa Chesterton.'

A car horn sounded. Vanessa snapped the bag shut, took a single deep breath, and hurried down the steps of her Victorian townhouse to the black cab waiting in the quiet tree-lined square beyond.

VANESSA CHESTERTON'S WISHES

The announcement of the winner of the Diamond Nib Award is always made between dessert and coffee. This may be so the nominees can enjoy their meal while there is still hope – provided they can control their nerves enough to swallow. Vanessa picks at her salmon roulade, although she is an old hand at such occasions and this year marks her fourth time on the shortlist. Her current tally is ten shortlists, fifteen longlists and zero awards, although her books are beloved of middle-class, middle-aged women in reading groups throughout Middle England.

At last, a little tug at her ankle. She retrieves her bag from under the table, wincing as the bodice stabs her underarm, then makes a crisp excuse and heads for the Ladies'.

'Nerves,' one of the spouses says, a little too loudly to pass unnoticed. 'Embarrassing to be nominated so many times and still not win.'

It is the agent's wife, a spindly, high-brow young woman and the brain behind a series of publicity events, including the mind-numbing reading sessions Vanessa recently endured at local care homes. She decides that the winner of the Diamond Nib will need a new agent – preferably a bachelor or someone with a fat, low-brow wife. She weaves her way across the ballroom, locks herself in a cubicle and opens her bag.

VANESSA CHESTERTON'S WISHES

'This is my year,' Vanessa told her laptop as she stared at the shortlist on the Diamond Nib website. She was sitting in her writer's study in an antique swivel chair surrounded by shelves of books and framed letters from celebrity fans. 'Everybody says it's my year. And I'm not going to lose out to that smirking upstart with a face full of pins.'

Essie assumed an arabesque on the keyboard, an incongruous combination with her tangerine hot pants and peephole bra. 'Just one little wish, Vanessa Chesterton, and everything shall be as you want it to be.'

Vanessa brushed Essie out of the way and opened her blog. 'If I take you to the award ceremony you'll fix it?'

'Easy as peasy.' Essie picked herself up and made a little curtsey.

Vanessa returns to the table, able now to enjoy her venison and spring vegetables. She engages in a light flirtation with the managing director's husband and even opens a benign discussion on blogging with the agent's wife.

Ty Floyde is seated two tables away – Vanessa has been keeping an eye on her all evening. Ty looks cool and relaxed, her head inclined towards her current partner, a beautiful female artist from Canada. They're so in love. You can read all about it in the gossip magazines and the newspapers – both the broadsheets and tabloids love Ty. So does the book-reading public; she's their tame lesbian, although Vanessa suspects that the Floyde woman's sexuality swings whichever way the wind of publicity is blowing.

Now she detects a glow in the air above Ty's head, a shimmering fall of dust. Vanessa glances quickly at the other assembled guests. Nobody else seems to have noticed, well nobody else would have been looking out for such a thing. Ty starts to fidget; agitated, she stares across the ballroom to the top table. Perhaps she sees a glimmer above the head judge; agitated, he breaks off in mid conversation and stares across at Ty.

Vanessa savours a mouthful of venison. And waits. After all, this won't be the first time, Essie has cleared someone out of the way of Vanessa's literary ambitions.

'Is it too much to ask for a little peace and quiet?' Vanessa turned to scowl at her study door which was failing to keep at bay the sound of her husband's enthusiasm for the Rugby World Cup.

Essie balanced a tiny candyfloss coloured rugby ball on her head as she performed a series of pirouettes across the desk.

'The match will soon be over, Vanessa Chesterton,' she trilled, waving her wand around her head, changing the ball from sugary pink through olive green and magenta before settling on a mustardy shade of yellow to match the pompoms on her bikini.

'And then he'll interrupt me to tell me the score. And he'll want to tell me about every single point. And who scored it and from where ...' Vanessa sank her head into her hands. 'If they

win he'll want to have sex tonight to celebrate. And if they lose he'll want to have sex to cheer himself up.'

'But sex is so nice.' Essie fluttered over and whispered in her ear. 'It's so warm and sticky and –'

'Not when you've got a deadline it isn't.' Vanessa flicked the fairy away. 'When you've got a deadline a husband is a right royal pain.'

Through the door came the sound of the final whistle closely followed by whoops of joy.

'Oh God. I just want some peace and quiet. Essie, make him leave me alone.'

'Do not worry, Vanessa Chesterton. Easy peasy for me to fix. You can finish writing your book in peace and quiet.'

Vanessa watches as Ty Floyde pushes back her chair. The beautiful sculptor gently touches Ty's arm, but is ignored. On the far side of the ballroom, the head judge stands and walks away from the top table. Both are heading for the back of the room, to the shadows that lie behind those long banners.

Minutes pass. Perhaps only moments. Vanessa realises she is holding her breath.

Then it happens. One of the stage spotlights seems to swivel on its hinges, swinging its beam onto Ty Floyde's banner. Everyone turns to look. Vanessa detects a glimmer of crimson dust falling from the balcony – as the banner crashes to the ground.

And Ty Floyde and the head judge are revealed. His trousers around his ankles. Her slim, tattooed legs wrapped around his waist.

VANESSA CHESTERTON'S WISHES

Vanessa listens to the collective intake of breath made by three hundred of the literary elite and covers her mouth with her hands to hide her smile. Essie must have used her 'obsessy-infatuaessy' spell.

'It's not fair!' Sixteen-year-old Vanessa lay sobbing on her bed.

Essie was practising entrechats in mid air, giggling at the sparks generated by her electric blue shell-suit. 'What is the matter, Vanessa Chesterton?'

Vanessa sniffed. 'Penny and Chrissie. All the boys at school chase after them. They've had dozens of boyfriends – I've only had one and I had to dump him because of his acne.'

'Poor Vanessa Chesterton.' Essie fiddled with the wand tangled in her silver spiral perm.

'You fix it for me!' Flushed and bright-eyed, Vanessa sat up. 'You can do it easily – give Penny and Chrissie pimples and make all the boys chase after me instead.'

Essie tugged the wand loose in a shimmering cloud of fairy dust. 'Easily peasily. Grant Vanessa Chesterton's wish!'

The chatter dies down long enough for Vanessa to collect her award. Ron Birch presents her with a lump of metal, less weighty and less finely cast than Vanessa had expected and she presents her cheek for him to kiss. She has her spontaneous speech ready. All the people she'd like to thank: her editor, her publisher, her agent, her family (although none are present) – she even adds Essie's name to pad out the list. Diplomatically Vanessa does not mention the absence of the head judge, nor the table recently vacated by Ty Floyde's party. Instead she earnestly articulates her desire for a world where women writers are empowered to let their work stand on its own merits, where nobody need submit to inappropriate sexual pressures to gain recognition. The audience applauds, cameras flash and Vanessa's happiness feels complete.

All around the ballroom of the Fortesque Hotel, little groups are holding animated discussions about the evening's events. Vanessa is escorted through the tables to a room set aside for interviews. As she passes, each group breaks off from their conversation to offer congratulations with handshaking and air-kisses; Vanessa acknowledges these with a gracious smile. But, away from the ballroom, she finds only a couple of journalists waiting.

She sees them one at a time, speaking expansively about the writing experience and how wonderful it is to receive such an honour after almost thirty years in the business. Vanessa lets herself be persuaded to speak of her divorce and the difficulty of combining personal relationships with an all-consuming passion such as writing, the sacrifices one must make for one's art. But she is less enthusiastic when the journalists want to discuss, at length, the evening's scandalous revelation.

The interviews are finished by eleven o'clock. As she walks through the lobby to her waiting taxi, all Vanessa can hear is excited chatter about the Ty

VANESSA CHESTERTON'S WISHES

Floyde love triangle. Typical! Why do things always go wrong for her?

'She mustn't know it was me. Don't ever let her know it was me.'

Twelve year old Vanessa swept fragments of porcelain into a dustpan: the remnants of Mum's precious dancing lady, all she had left of her own mother who died so suddenly seven years before.

'But don't you want me to ... ' Essie hovered a few feet away, ' ... mend it?' she whispered. 'It would be easy pea–'

Vanessa reached up and grabbed the fairy in her fist, squeezing until her hair turned from deep purple to grey. 'Just do what I say.,' she hissed. 'I wish that Mum never ever finds out it was me.' Her mouth twisted as she remembered an earlier confrontation with her father. 'Make her believe it was Dad.'

Essie wriggled free, hitching up puce harem pants. She screwed up her face and twirled her wand round and round above her head, 'Grant Vanessa Chesterton's wish. Grant Vanessa Chesterton's wish ...'

Vanessa lets herself into the house and locks the front door. She shuts herself in her study, puts her evening bag down on the desk and positions the Diamond Nib statuette in a space she has cleared ready. She sinks into her antique writer's chair, wincing as the bodice lacerates her skin, and opens her laptop.

VANESSA CHESTERTON'S WISHES

Ty Floyde's escapades have gone viral. On the whole the response is sympathetic, blame falling like an axe on the head judge for abusing his position. The beautiful Canadian sculptor has been quick to forgive, of course. Even Hollywood is showing an interest, scenting a profit in Ty's now disqualified book. Only two articles mention the actual winner of the Diamond Nib – one of these names the author as Veronica Chessington.

Vanessa reaches for a bottle of malt whisky and takes a sizable slug. She picks up her evening bag and smashes it on the desk, again and again, creating a storm of red sequins. Then she hurls the bag at the Diamond Nib award. The statuette topples from the shelf and the bag falls open on the floor.

'I hate Grannie!'

Five-year-old Vanessa stomped down to the bottom of her grandparents' garden. Checking that she couldn't be seen from the house, she pulled off a handful of strawberries and squashed them under her white satin ballet slippers.

'And I hate ballet!' she hissed. 'I wish I had a friend all to myself. Someone who plays whatever I want, and does whatever I want and never ever ever says NO.'

'Can I be your friend?' came a little voice. And out from behind the strawberry plants stepped a tiny fairy with frizzy red hair, a green tutu and orange jelly sandals.

Vanessa burst out laughing. 'You look silly.'

'I can look as silly as you like,' the fairy replied eagerly.

'Can you grant wishes?'

VANESSA CHESTERTON'S WISHES

'Easy as peasy!'
'Well I wish my Grannie —'
'First you have to give me a name. If I'm going to be your fairy, I have to have a name.'
'Essie Bessie Big Bum!'
The little fairy's smile drooped. 'It has to be a flower name. Or a plant.'
'Alright, Essie Stinkweed!' Vanessa laughed. 'And you must call me Vanessa Chesterton.' She thought for a moment, then solemnly pronounced: 'I wish my Grannie can never ever tell me off again.'
Essie Stinkweed pulled a fairy wand from her purple knickers. She screwed up her face in concentration, raised the wand above her head and, making little circles in the air muttered to herself, 'Grant Vanessa Chesterton's wish.'

Vanessa remembers how that wish worked out. And she remembers others. Her mother screaming accusations about a broken ornament and her father slamming the door as he left. Herself running scared and sweating all the way home from school pursued by a pack of hormonally-charged teenaged boys. And how the peace Vanessa craved to finish her book had been achieved by dispatching her husband into the arms of the divorcee next door.

'Essie Stinkweed!' she snarls. 'I should have known you'd mess it up. What sort of fairy are you anyway? How did I ever end up with such a stupid, pathetic excuse for a fairy?'

VANESSA CHESTERTON'S WISHES

Essie climbs delicately out of the battered evening bag, smoothing her crumpled wings. She examines her reflection in the patent shine of her thigh high boots. She appears to think carefully about Vanessa's question.

'I am here to do whatever you want, Vanessa Chesterton. To play whatever you want and to never ever ever say No. I am here to grant whatever you wish for.'

'Then you're a ... a ... a rubbish fairy!'

Essie performs a series of grand jeté in mid-air.

'Granting wishes is easy as peasy. Any old fairy can do it. *Making* wishes – that's the bit that matters.'

She lands in a perfect arabesque on Vanessa's desk.

'If *I* am a rubbish fairy, Vanessa Chesterton, it is because *you* always make such rubbish wishes.'

And Essie finishes with a beautiful curtsey.

The Burning Girl

Looking at the house was like seeing his mother again, the same uncompromising, urban respectability. The property itself was a no-nonsense double fronted villa set in a quarter of an acre of lawn and leylandii, walls painted the same decorous pale green, bay windows demure with floral lace kept spotless with white vinegar. Just as it was last month when his mother was still living there. Or the month before when there was no hint she wouldn't be there for another decade. From the outside the house was maintaining standards and, give or take a conifer or two, it looked just the same as it had for more than sixty years.

Ron parked his cream cabriolet outside the garage and, leaving his overnight bag and a large cardboard box on the back seat, crunched back down the gravel to close the gates behind him. He bent to pull up a dandelion that had sneaked in beside the fence, this single weed the only sign of negligence on the part of the young man whose father and grandfather had mown, mulched and weeded the gardens of Magnolia Road. Of course, Ron mused as he removed his shoes in the hall and placed them neatly on the rack beside the front door, there had been inevitable changes over the years – central heating, the ubiquitous white-framed double glazing – yet the parquet flooring still shone with a menacing gleam and the air smarted with the smell of lavender polish.

He opened the kitchen door. Four chairs stood at a table scrubbed spotless but for a little blue stain on the side of the wood. Ron recalled his homework neatly set out on that table, complete with slide rule and dictionary. He pictured filling his fountain pen from the pot of blue ink as Mum placed a glass of milk and a digestive biscuit on a willow pattern plate beside his books. He smiled as he remembered the time he'd asked for cola and Mum replied firmly, 'We are not Americans, Ronald.'

He and Connie had laughed about it at break the next day. 'Dare you to ask for pale ale tonight,' she said.

Ron checked his watch: ten to eleven, the estate agent would be arriving at any time. He unlocked the back door and pulled up the kitchen blind to show off the sunny veranda and a lawn smooth as Axminster. Then he passed through the rest of the ground floor rooms opening doors and drawing curtains.

Postponing further memories for a more convenient time, Ron waited in the sitting room, standing so as to not un-plump the cushions, hands resting on the top of Dad's cocktail bar, a nineteen-sixties DIY project which lived on long after Dad as a reminder that he had, at least, been good with his hands.

The estate agent was a pretty young thing, disguising her inexperience within a formal navy suit and silk scarf. Mum would have found no reason to disapprove, although she would have preferred a man.

'Mr Birch?' The estate agent extended her hand. She looked down at his socks. 'Oh – should I take my shoes off?'

'No need. It's just habit with me. Please come through.'

Ron led the estate agent into the sitting room where she sat down on the sofa, looking from Dad's bar to Mum's display cabinet with its pristinely positioned china and silver-framed photographs. So many snaps of Ron and so few of his father.

What was it Connie had said? 'That's a heavy weight of love to carry on your own. Maybe I'm the lucky one – no parents, just a mean old aunt who doesn't care if I live or die.'

THE BURNING GIRL

And Connie had taken the sting out of her words by laughing. He loved it when she laughed.

'It's my mother's house,' he explained to the estate agent. 'She died recently.'

'Oh. I'm so sorry. Was she very old?'

Meaning, Ron thought, I'm probably old enough to be your grandpa so she must have been ancient. 'Nineties,' he replied. 'Quite old.' He gave the estate agent a carefully crooked smile that brought a little blush to her cheeks despite the difference in their ages.

Ron took a seat in his usual chair and they went through the basic details: detached family house, four beds, three receps, and so on.

'The house was built in the 1950s,' Ron explained. 'My parents were the first owners. Not the most elegant of periods, architecturally speaking, but spacious. It probably needs updating – ensuite bathroom and so on.'

'Oh yes,' the estate agent nodded as she swept an index finger across her electronic tablet. 'Essential in a property this size. And, of course, when the same person lives in a house all those years the décor can become a bit …'

Ron helped her out. 'Cryogenic?'

'I'm sorry?'

'Frozen in time.'

'Oh …' the estate agent's mouth turned up at one corner before blossoming into a smile. 'Excuse me, Mr Birch. Have I seen you somewhere before?'

'I've been on the TV a bit over the past few weeks.' Ron turned slightly to maximise his profile. 'Interviews. My book's just been made into a film.'

'Oh, of course. Oh wow!' she exclaimed. 'Ron Birch – you were on Film Talk. *The Burning Girl.* We went to see it last night. It's fantastic. I cried my eyes out when she died. Was she really based on someone you knew at school – '

'Glad you enjoyed it.' Ron ushered her into the hall. 'Perhaps you'd like to start downstairs.'

Ron left the estate agent to measure up the downstairs rooms: kitchen, sitting room, dining room, and that awkwardly shaped space at the back of the house that Mum had assigned as Dad's workroom to keep him from under their feet, the only place in the house where smoking was tolerated. He climbed the stairs, running his hand along the varnished banister, wondering even now if it would have made a good slide. At the top he hesitated and glanced down into the hall, pushing back fractured memories of Connie and Mum, of voices raised. Later, he told himself. There would be time later.

He walked along the galleried landing, opening up the rooms one by one, pulling back curtains and gathering up a dead fly or two: the spare room, the small box bedroom, the family bathroom that smelt of lily of the valley air-freshener. When he reached his mother's room, Ron hesitated, edging the door open as though he might surprise Mum putting her face on. But the room, with its white rose wallpaper and peach satin eiderdown, was still and silent. Only the scent remained, a blend of face powder and eau de cologne that no distance of miles or years would ever let him forget.

'Your mother always smells the same,' Connie had said. 'That pretty, made-up sort of smell nice mummies are supposed to have.' She laughed, but it wasn't a laugh he liked.

Ron stood beside Mum's dressing table in the bay window and looked at his car in the driveway, at the bag and box on the back seat.

'This must be the master bedroom?' The estate agent stood in the doorway. 'It's a very good size. You could easily fit an ensuite in here. Maybe even a walk-in wardrobe.'

She joined Ron at the window.

'Oh, what a view! You can see everything up and down the road from here.'

'Not much got past my mother.'

'And more pictures!' The estate agent picked up a mahogany-framed photo of Ron smiling like a matinee idol. 'Wow – you were gorgeous!' She gave a little laugh and blushed again.

Connie once said, 'Ron, you're the handsomest boy in the school. But you're like a piece of art in a museum and your mother's the curator. We can admire you – but we mustn't touch.'

The estate agent's cheeks grew pinker. 'She ... your mother ... must have been very proud of you. Especially with the film and everything.'

'She died just before it came out.'

'Oh, what a shame.'

'Perhaps,' Ron said. Perhaps not, he thought.

'Have you written lots of other books?'

'A few.' He pre-empted her next question, 'None of the others have been made into films.'

'Well this one's brilliant. That horrible headmaster. And that scene where she's up on the roof as the school burns down – wow!'

'I wish I could burn it down. I'd set fire to the whole stinking, heretical place and watch it burn. With him in it.' Connie hadn't laughed at all when she said that. Ron was scared she was going to cry.

The estate agent took some measurements, then they left Mum's room. Ron opened the last door across the landing and flicked a light switch.

'This is my room.'

Dust free, preserved: the room where Ron had spent tens of thousands of childhood hours – and a good many adult hours as well. A matching headboard and bedside tables framed a single divan made up with crisp linen. A bookcase, Dad's handiwork, was stacked with box files and topped off with a row of leather-bound classics. Beneath the window stood a desk, overly grand in both size and style, its surface covered with an array of books by Ron Birch.

Ron was caught between embarrassment and nostalgia.

'Another good-sized room,' the estate agent said, tapping at her tablet. She walked up to the desk and ran her fingers over the books. 'Wow. Did you write all these?'

Above the desk, peach velvet curtains were closed so tightly that they overlapped across the window sealing the room from the outside world. Ron tugged them open.

'Oh, what a lovely view of the garden,' the estate agent declared. 'That lawn must have been great for football.'

Ron remembered his mother's verdict on football: 'Ball games, Ronald, are for boys who lack academic aspiration.'

'My mother,' he said, 'liked the garden laid to lawn.'

Connie's interpretation was different. 'Your mother distrusts anything that doesn't grow in a straight line. She wants the world mown and pruned and domesticated. Pity,' she laughed as she perched on Ron's bedroom windowsill, 'I could do with a bit of ivy to hang onto.'

The estate agent picked up a book. 'Is this one of yours?'

'No, that's one of Percy Bysshe Shelley's.'

'St Jude's Grammar School Prize for Poetry. Awarded to Ron Birch Summer Term 1958. So you were always good at writing.'

Connie had pulled the book from her satchel and thrust it at him. 'I don't want anything that creep's touched. Your mother's desperate for you to win — so we'll write your name on a new bookplate and paste it over mine. Then everybody's happy.'

Ron took the book and closed the cover. He pointed out of the window, away beyond the garden to a building in the distance, its roof and upper floors visible above the trees and houses.

'That's St Jude's.'

The estate agent moved closer to the window. 'The school that burned down?'

'Don't confuse fiction with reality. St Jude's Grammar is still standing. *The Burning Girl* is just a story. Built on a handful of memories.'

Memories of Connie here in his room, her eyes ablaze, her soft, clever lips raging against the world. Connie crying in her sleep, her beautiful hair tangled across his starched pillowcase. Creeping down the stairs; easing back the bolts; the sound of her feet running across the gravel. The light under Mum's door when he tiptoed back to bed.

The estate agent cleared her throat and Ron pushed his memories aside again.

He watched from the back door as the estate agent stepped out into the garden. Every corner could be seen from the house, there were no nooks or secret paths where anything could be safely hidden away. Perhaps, Ron thought, nothing could ever truly be said to be safe or secret, unless you locked it up inside of you and swallowed the key.

Mum had never once mentioned Ron's masterpiece, *The Burning Girl*, the one book of which he was honestly proud. He wondered if she'd ever read it. She must have known the film was coming out, although it was not spoken of between them. Ultimately, Mum circumvented that dark corner by dying precisely a month before the premiere.

'*Your mother's a very determined woman,*' Connie had said.

The estate agent was hopeful of an early sale. She was more relaxed now, smiling and stroking her hair as she talked. Ron considered inviting her to dinner, but he knew he'd prove a disappointment, if not that night then within a week or a year. Instead he fetched his bag and the large cardboard box from the backseat of his car and signed his name in black marker pen across the crimson sky of an oversized publicity poster.

'I've got plenty more,' he said, rolling it up and handing it to the estate agent.

'Oh wow,' she said. 'Thank you.' And she kissed his cheek.

Ron walked the young woman out to the road and watched as she drove away. He returned to the house and, without removing his shoes, climbed the stairs to his bedroom. Shutting the door behind him, Ron sat at his desk, looked out of the window, and remembered.

Connie. Crazy beautiful Connie with her long wild hair and her long wild thoughts. Climbing up to his room in the middle of the night. Sitting on his desk as they forged the dedication in the poetry prize. Laughing her lovely laugh, a little too loudly for Ron's peace of mind, and whispering how she'd sneaked into the Head's office and picked the lock on his desk drawer to steal the bookplate. How she slipped behind the curtains when she heard his flat feet in the corridor outside, climbed out of the window, then ran away across the playing field as soon as the coast was clear. Ron never knew what to believe when Connie told a story; her imagination was, in her own words, 'free voyaging with no anchor to the truth'. But, then again, she had climbed up to his first floor bedroom window using only the drainpipe and sills.

'You ought to be more careful,' he told her, under his breath so Mum wouldn't hear. 'One day he'll catch you and you'll be in so much trouble. You might even get expelled.'

Connie laughed the brittle laugh Ron hated. 'He'd never expel me. He enjoys our little 'tête-à-têtes' too much. The creep gets a boner every time he reaches for the cane.'

She pulled a pack of cigarettes from her satchel. 'Smoke?'

'No, I ... No, don't! Mum will smell it.' Ron looked at the silver lighter in Connie's hand, 'Where did you get that?'

She flicked the flint wheel and stared into the flame. 'Off his desk. Look, there's an inscription: Presented by His Worship the Mayor.' Connie slipped her trophy away again, climbed off the desk and stretched out across Ron's bed.

'Can I stay here for a bit? My aunt's a very light sleeper – it's safer to sneak in tomorrow morning and pretend I just got up.'

Ron felt his pyjama trousers stir. 'OK,' he said.

THE BURNING GIRL

He waited for Connie to invite him to join her on the bed, but she fell asleep, her beautiful hair rambling over his pillow – unmown, unpruned. Her school uniform was crumpled, her stockings badly darned. Hands stained with blue ink, nails bitten, flesh chewed. Everyone at school said she was bad news. But she was also the poet Ron already suspected he would never be. He looked at the girl lying on his bed and wondered if the trembling he felt was love.

Ron saw there was mud on his counterpane. He carefully slipped the shoes off Connie's feet, thinking how he'd like to smooth out the wrinkles in her stockings. Her skirt had ridden up a little, to just above her knees. Bad news. Connie was more than a year older than him, almost sixteen. Bad girl. Hands trembling, Ron eased the skirt higher, then a little higher, until he could see her suspenders.

Silently at first, then with little gulps for air, Connie was crying in her sleep. Ron let go of the skirt and she curled up like a baby animal, her hair falling across her face, sticking among the tears and snot. Ron backed away and sat at his desk. He stared out of the window towards St Jude's in the distance and wished her gone.

His mother must have known. At the first light of dawn, Ron had panicked and woken Connie, hurrying her out of the front door as quietly as he could. Of course Mum must have known, but it was never mentioned. Nor was the fact that Connie returned the next night and this time she rang the doorbell.

THE BURNING GIRL

Ron was sitting up in bed reading a leather-bound copy of 'Great Expectations', a gift from his mother. He glanced at his alarm clock: a quarter to ten, too late for any respectable caller. He heard Mum speaking, but couldn't catch her words. What was it Connie had said about Mum's voice? He'd used the image in one of his poems: 'Your mother's words are like snow. So quiet as they fall all around you, you never realise the danger until your heart is frozen.'

Ron's door was not quite closed. He propped his book on the bedside table, being careful to not bend the spine, and crept across the room to listen.

Mum's voice was quiet, soft and cold. 'Ronald is in bed.'

Connie's was ragged and rising. 'I need to see him, Mrs Birch.'

Had he heard Dad's workroom door open and close again? Ron slithered out onto the landing, keeping low so he couldn't be seen.

'I cannot imagine, young woman, what business you could have with my son at this hour.'

Ron could hear the effort behind Connie's politeness. 'I know it's late and I'm very sorry. But I've got to talk to Ron.'

'Ronald is in — '

'Then I'll go up.'

'You will not.'

Ron crawled along the landing and peered around the head of the stairs.

They were standing face to face. Two females of similar height and build. One on the doorstep, fidgeting from foot to foot, school blouse untucked and skirt askew, curls slick with tears. The other wrapped in a floral housecoat, her hair

211

respectably rollered, and her feet solid as a sentry's on the parquet flooring.

'Look, Mrs Birch. Something terrible ... something's happened. I need Ron. You don't understand – '

'Oh I understand, Constance. I know all about you. What your poor aunt has to put up with. You might be a ... a dirty girl, but I will not let you contaminate my son. And I will not have you in my house. Stay away from Ronald or I will inform your headmaster.'

'Headmaster?' Connie nearly choked on the word. 'Oh you inform him, Mrs Birch. You tell him what a nasty, dirty girl I am. And you ask him about the nasty, dirty thing he made me do.'

Then Connie had laughed; she had thrown back her head and laughed till Ron wanted to put his hands over his ears or round her throat to stop the noise. He stumbled against the balustrade and she looked up, looked straight to where he was hiding, and screamed his name, 'Ron!'

Ron shrank back into the shadows at the top of the stairs. Mum reached out her hand, pushed Connie off the step and slammed the door shut.

Did Connie see him? Ron would never know.

He stared out of his bedroom window, straining his eyes on St Jude's still standing beyond the trees. He'd seen the glow of the fire and heard the sirens in the night. He could still picture the headlines in the local paper. Still smell the smoking ruins of the Headmaster's study, and recall the charred aftertaste of relief that the Head himself had been miles away

THE BURNING GIRL

that night, personal guest of the Mayor at a civic banquet. Over weeks and months as the school was repaired Ron listened to the gossip, to talk of police and ambulances, of terrible burns. Then to whispers about the Asylum. Until, at last, Connie was mentioned no more.

As for that image, that iconic image blazing out from all the posters – the girl, her hair on fire, posed, as if crucified, high on the roof of the school – Ron never saw her burn. He hid in his room, shut his door and pulled the curtains so close they overlapped.

Years later, following his first divorce, he moved back home for a while and sat hour after hour in his old room staring at his bed and out of that window. When *The Burning Girl* demanded he tell her story, Ron, the writer, asked himself:

How would Connie have envisaged the scene?

And from the shadows locked inside him, Connie struck an iconic pose.

Ron looked out of his bedroom window and wondered how his life would have been if he'd gone downstairs that night and stood up to his mother. How had Connie's life been? Perhaps it was better never to know.

He got up from his desk and walked slowly down the stairs and into the kitchen. To where the cardboard box from the film studio sat next to his overnight bag. He took a carton of thumb tacks from

THE BURNING GIRL

his bag, then unrolled a poster and pinned it like a cloth over the kitchen table. He pinned another to the back door. The cupboards were harder to penetrate, but Ron drove the tacks home with his mother's rolling pin.

He papered the sitting room walls with images of Connie, standing like a crucifix on the roof of the burning school, her hair aflame. Then he turned to the furniture. The wood of Dad's bar was yielding, but Mum's glass cabinet was framed with a stubborn metal, so Ron fetched a roll of sticky tape from his bag. When that was finished, he began on the dining room, then the hall, working in a creative dream fuelled by the chemical odour of the freshly unrolled posters.

Ron worked his way up the stairs, whistling bars of the film score, building to a crescendo as he reached the landing. He attached a poster to each door and carefully folded another to place a *Burning Girl* in the bathtub. In his own room he pinned images of Connie to his wardrobe and shelves before gently laying a poster across the bed, weighting the corners with books from his desk. By teatime he was almost done.

Scooping up the remaining posters, tacks and sticky tape, Ron carried them to his mother's room. He piled them up on the bed and stretched his stiff shoulders in readiness for this last effort. He pinned his way around the room until not a single wallpaper rose remained. He taped images of Connie across the bay window, blocking the view of the road and hiding away all those smiling testaments of filial duty. Until there was only one poster left.

Sweeping the last of the thumb tacks and sticky tape onto the floor, Ron unrolled the final poster across Mum's bed, but it curled up again as soon as he let go. He tried securing it with the tacks, but couldn't get purchase in the eiderdown. He used sticky tape, but the satin was so slippery the tape wouldn't hold and the corners of the poster slid away when he tried weighting them with books. Ron stopped whistling and realised his stomach was growling and his throat was dry.

In the kitchen, he drank water straight from the tap and finished up a packet of digestives as he searched through cupboards and drawers. Frustrated, he wandered into the hall and came face to face with Connie on the poster he'd pinned to Dad's workroom door. Ron turned the handle and stepped inside.

The workroom was a hoard of old boxes and tins stacked on shelves supported by bare brackets. On his father's workbench, against the far wall, sat an ashtray and Dad's old brass lighter. The room smelled quite unlike the rest of the house: of wood shavings and old emulsion, of turpentine and stale cigarettes. Ron pocketed the lighter and scanned the shelves, reading rows of faded labels printed in his father's cramped hand, until he found the very thing.

Back upstairs, Ron painted the eiderdown with a sticky mess of ancient, but still pungent, glue and pasted Connie across his mother's bed.

The landing and the hall downstairs were dark now, every window covered by a poster. Ron took Dad's lighter from his pocket and walked through the house flicking the flame on and off, seeing it reflect in the sheen of the paper. He held the lighter close to Connie's face, and watched the fire gleaming in the dark of her eyes. For a moment, Ron imagined touching the flame to the picture and joining Connie in her glorious act of rebellion. For just a moment he was other than his mother had made him. Then he flipped the lid of the lighter closed.

All around him the house was ablaze with images of *The Burning Girl*.

What was it Mum had said? '… dirty girl … I will not have you in my house.'

Ron stood in the hall, planting his feet squarely on his mother's parquet flooring, and imagined a sound he loved. Somewhere, in this world or the next, Connie was laughing.

Author's note

When I wrote the first story in this collection, *The Woman Who Never Did,* two of the characters didn't want to leave me. One of them was the protagonist, Connie, and I knew that one day I would return to her story and go back in time to fill in the gaps. The other was Jean and I wanted to write more about her straight away.

Jean walked out of *The Woman Who Never Did* and into her own story, *Gloria.* And that was what kept happening. Each time I finished a story, a character, or something a little more obscure, would continue on. Sometimes they walked into their own story; sometimes they became the catalyst in someone else's.

So it went on until the final piece in the collection completed the circle and took me back to the beginning. Back to *The Woman Who Never Did.*

This is my first collection of short stories. My aim has been to distil a full, life-sized story into something you can read in a coffee-break, or on the bus to work, or waiting to collect the children from school. I hope you enjoy them.

If you would like to find out more about my writing, please visit www.jeneferheap.wordpress.com.

Acknowledgements

I've had so much support and encouragement in producing this book that I have a long list of people to thank.

Thank you, Catherine White and Sophie Whitley-Flavell, for patiently reading every single word of my stories (often many times over) and giving me your honest and constructive feedback – even when I didn't always want to hear it. And thank you, Philippa Mitchell, for being the first to read my book in its entirety and only laughing where you were meant to.

Thank you to all my creative writing tutors for teaching me The Rules; and especially to Michael Wyndham Thomas for giving me the confidence to break those rules when I needed to.

Thank you to Liz Cheetham and Anita Reeves, my learning companions through three years of study – you made learning such fun. Thank you to Andy Killeen and the PoW-WoW writers' group (www.powwowwritersgroup.co.uk) for including my stories in your anthologies. And thank you also to the many other writers I've met over the years whose talent and generosity of spirit have been such an inspiration

Thank you to my editor, Katharine de Souza (www.katharinedsouza.co.uk), for having real insight into what I was trying to say and the wisdom to help me find a better way to say it.

Thank you to all the ladies in our book group for recommending such an exciting range of styles and genres and for giving me the perfect excuse to leave the ironing and pick up a book instead (sorry but I have to read this – it's book group tonight).

Thank you, Colette and Mike Long, for your very timely help in the final push to publication and for making me look so nice in my photo.

A very big thank you to *Good Housekeeping* and the panel of judges who awarded me first place in your annual short story competition – when you printed my story *Wendy's Tiger* in your magazine you made me believe I could be a writer and inspired me to be patient and persevere when life got in the way.

And last, but very far from least, thank you to my family. To my parents, Donald and Molly Rosser, and my sister, Susan Screech, for filling our home and my childhood with books and stories, you are the foundation of my ambitions to write stories of my own. To my husband, Colin, for your love, your support and for having faith in my ability to write even when I haven't. And to my children, Kitty and Jim, for being proud of me and telling everyone that Mummy is a writer.

Made in the USA
Charleston, SC
13 January 2016